"You can lea
Margot said politely, the
edge of frustration coloring
her tone.

Slowly Rand smiled, amusement dancing in his eyes as he stood leaning against one of the support pillars. He looked cool and controlled.

"I don't think so, Margot. We have some unfinished business between us, and now is as good a time as any to get it resolved, wouldn't you say?"

"Is that why you came? To talk about the past?"

"Why I came isn't as important as why I'm staying."

Before she could even think of a response, he lowered his head and covered her mouth with his.

Shocked, Margot felt the past and present merge until she had no idea where she was. Rand's lips moved against hers as passionately as ever, as familiar as her own heartbeat. The world spun and Margot almost forgot the years that had separated them, the tragedy that had ripped their world apart.

Dear Reader,

Welcome to BEAUFORT BRIDES, a trilogy about three sisters who untangle a web of deceit from the past and discover that the solving of this puzzle leads to a gorgeous bridegroom and a glorious wedding for each of them!

My three heroines, Margot, Shelby and Georgia, are all very different, yet their qualities complement each other perfectly. Margot has a strong sense of responsibility, Shelby is quiet and shy and Georgia is outrageous and daring. I like to think that I have something of each of these women in myself!

I had a wonderful time developing stories for these remarkable sisters and the extra-special men in their lives. Together, they determine to follow their hearts until the truth about their father is revealed. I invite you to come and see....

Barbara McMahon

Look for Shelby's story, A MOTHER FOR MOLLIE, coming in August 2000, and Georgia's story, GEORGIA'S GROOM, coming in September 2000.

MARRYING MARGOT

Barbara McMahon

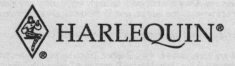

TORONTO • NEW YORK • LONDON
AMSTERDAM • PARIS • SYDNEY • HAMBURG
STOCKHOLM • ATHENS • TOKYO • MILAN • MADRID
PRAGUE • WARSAW • BUDAPEST • AUCKLAND

ISBN 0-373-15858-0

MARRYING MARGOT

First North American Publication 2000.

Visit us at www.eHarlequin.com

Printed in U.S.A.

COVETING MARGOT

CHAPTER ONE

THE insistent rapping on the brass knocker added urgency to Margot's rapid crossing of the wide foyer. Her stocking-clad feet made no sound on the cold expanse of marble. She ignored the discomfort. Her heart felt just as cold. She thought the last mourner had departed only moments ago, had they forgotten something? She was tired—too tired to deal with much more. The entire last six weeks had been emotionally draining. Today's funeral had been the capper. She had thought she'd melt in the unseasonably warm February sun. Mississippi was supposed to cool down just a bit in winter. Of course, nothing else had gone right over the last few weeks, why should she have expected anything different today? She longed to crawl into bed and forget everything!

Opening the door, she tried for a semblance of a smile. Only to have her efforts freeze when she saw the man standing there. The last person on the face of the earth she expected to see— Rand Marstall!

For a second, a tidal wave of emotions surged through her. Disbelief, anger, sorrow and hurt combined with a hint of disbelieving joy. She stared at her husband, unable to say a word. What was he doing here? Or were her eyes playing tricks on her? Was she losing her mind? After ignoring her for five years, was he truly standing on the doorstep large as life and twice as sexy?

"Hello, Margot," he said in a voice she'd never forgotten. "Going somewhere?" He looked at her black dress, the single strand of pearls, the neatly sleeked-back hair, his glance giving nothing away.

Slowly her eyes traced him from his dark conservatively cut hair to the tips of his shiny wing tips as if she sought to imprint every detail on her mind. He looked older, of course. And harder, like tempered steel. She had an eye for fabric and style—his suit would cost more than her monthly rent, his shoes almost as much. Were his shoulders broader than she remembered? He looked toned, healthy and as successful as he'd always wished.

Success, she remembered instantly, had been vitally important to him. Obviously he'd attained what he wanted.

But at what cost?

For a moment a sharp pain almost buckled

her knees. She gripped the doorknob tighter, depending on it as if it were a lifeline. It had been *years* since their brief seven-month marriage had ended. If someone had asked her yesterday, she would have sworn she was over Rand Marstall. Had put him and their life together behind her forever.

Her reaction at seeing him disproved that. Resentfully she glared at him. How dare he come waltzing back as if he had a right. Like he had any rights. He'd forfeited them all long ago. Yet, one look at the man and all the old feelings began to resurface. The primary ones being hurt and betrayal—and an overwhelming sadness from the death of a dream.

The story of her life, apparently.

"This is a surprise, Rand. What are you doing here?" she asked as he continued to stand on the wide veranda. She wanted to slam the door in his face as if that would slam a lid on the caldron of memories that bubbled below the surface. But proper behavior, drilled into her from infancy, kept her from acting so rudely.

"I came to see you."

The control in his voice was nothing like the hot passionate tone he'd once used in the dark of night, when it had been the two of them against the world. Before he'd let her down. Before he'd ignored her, blamed her, turned from her to make work the most important focus of his life—even more important than his own wife.

"I don't want to see you." It sounded childish. She didn't care; she only wanted him gone. Hadn't she endured enough?

"You've made that perfectly clear over the years. It's time to—"

"Who is it, Margot?" Shelby entered the foyer from the living room. She, too, was dressed in black. Her high heels clicked on the marble floor. "Well, I declare. Rand!" She stopped and stared at the man in surprise. "We didn't expect you."

"Shelby." He nodded briefly in acknowledgment, his eyes taking in the difference between the sisters, and the similarities. Margot was older by eighteen months, but several inches shorter than her tall, slender younger sister. Both had deep blue eyes, but Margot's hair was a dark brown while Shelby's was a rich dark auburn.

"What are you doing here?" Shelby asked, glancing between her sister and Rand. If she sensed any tension, she gave no sign.

Margot started to turn, wondering if her knees would support her if she let go of the door. Wishing she dare slam it shut, bolt it and pretend she'd never seen the man. She did not need this today of all days!

"I asked him the same thing. Apparently he's here to see me," she said irritated. She'd thought the worst was over, that there'd be some peace at last. Was she never to have a moment's serenity again?

Shelby smiled in polite welcome. "We didn't expect you, Rand. How did you hear?"

Rand glanced from one sister to the other, narrowing his eyes in assessment. Suddenly things began to add up. He had not risen as swiftly as he had in the shipping industry by ignoring obvious clues.

He looked at Margot. "A death in the family?"

She nodded. "Grandmother."

"Damn." He'd come to see Margot, to force the issue they'd been ignoring for five years. Their marriage was over and it was time to formally end it. He had the preliminary divorce papers in his pocket. Normally his timing was perfect. Apparently not today.

"That explains your opening the door," he said. "Harriet would never have let that menial task be performed by a member of her illustrious family."

"I don't need your sarcasm, Rand.

Grandmother's help was given the week off. Of course I opened the door.''

''We're the only ones here. Come in,'' Shelby said. ''No sense letting all the cool air escape. It's hot as Hades outside. Early February and it feels like July! I thought I'd melt at the cemetery.''

Rand glanced at Margot—raising an eyebrow he waited for her to speak. He was startled to find her looking so wan and thin.

What had she been doing to herself over the last five years? Besides ignoring his attempts to get in touch with her? For a moment, he felt a hint of concern. Ruthlessly damping down on the unexpected feeling, he reminded himself why he'd come.

She'd had endless opportunities to contact him, to respond to his attempts to reach her. Her refusal to deal with him made her position crystal clear, and relieved him of any responsibility. Once she signed the papers, once the divorce went through, he need never feel concern for her again.

''Come in, then,'' she said reluctantly. ''I can't imagine why you chose today to show up.''

''When did Harriet die?'' Rand asked stepping inside and pushing the door.

Margot released the knob before she came in

contact with Rand, glad to see her knees worked fine. Only, with the door shut, the foyer seemed to shrink. Taking a step backward to put some distance between them, she frowned as she studied him. She didn't want Rand here. Didn't want to see him. And especially didn't want to feel the emotions his presence unleashed. There was enough on her plate now with her grandmother's death, Margot didn't need anything more.

"She died Thursday night. We just came from the funeral a little while ago. You missed the wake," Shelby said.

"What are y'all doing out here?" Georgia Beaufort stopped in the doorway and looked at the group. Her face lit with delight when she spotted Rand. Spontaneously she dashed across the floor and flung her arms around his neck exuberantly. "Rand! What a surprise! How wonderful!" Almost as tall as Shelby, Georgia looked totally unlike either of her two older sisters. Her ash-blond hair seemed at odds with the darker shades of her sisters'. But her smile was pure Beaufort, along with the deep blue eyes.

Margot watched, wishing she dare yank her younger sister away from the man and send her to her room. Georgia had always had a warm spot in her heart for Rand. Five years ago at seventeen, she had thought him totally romantic. Even now, after all that had transpired, she obviously continued to harbor warm feelings for the man.

Traitor, Margot thought. Then felt stricken. It wasn't her sister's fault she liked the man. Georgia didn't know the entire story. Her heart hadn't been broken, her life left in tatters.

And whose fault was it that she didn't know, a voice inside asked. She had never told the full story to anyone but her grandmother. Had things been different, had Rand followed her, contacted her years ago—

No! She refused to even think along those lines. He hadn't. End of story.

Except—for a split second Margot wished she could feel the warmth of his arms holding her, could lean against his hard body, draw on his strength. Just once more. She was so tired. And she felt so alone.

"So did you come to help with settling the estate?" Georgia asked excitedly. "We've missed you, haven't we?" Her gaze swept the others in the foyer.

"No!" Margot said quickly, glaring at Rand. "There's no need for you to be here. We've managed fine without you for years. We can certainly manage another death in the family without your help."

Georgia looked stunned. Shelby blinked, her

watchful gaze moving back and forth between her sister and Rand. No one ever mentioned that. Not in all the years since Margot had returned home.

The tightening in Rand's jaw was the only sign he heard. His eyes gave no indication what he thought of her salvo. "I came to see you, to talk to you. The timing may be inconvenient, but I'm not leaving until we do."

Something held back the scathing words he'd planned to say once he saw Margot face-to-face. He'd had years to refine them, until they conveyed exactly his contempt for her actions. Granted, he had not behaved admirably under the circumstances. But her behavior had been inexcusable.

Seeing her again, realizing her grandmother had just died, he couldn't tell her precisely what he thought. Even he had some sensibilities—though he was sure she would disagree. Time enough in the next day or two, when things settled down, to attend to business. If she thought he'd give up now that he was here, she didn't know him. He'd stay until he got the situation settled.

If needed, he'd keep in touch with the office via phone. It wasn't as if he made a habit of being away. But now that he was face-to-face with his wife for the first time in five years, he was taking no chances. They would settle the matter before he left, inconvenient time or not!

"I'd say the timing is inconvenient. I still can't imagine why you drove all this way. What do you want? Why today? Why not phone?" Margot wanted to open the door in a sweeping gesture, and make him leave. She knew she couldn't force him to do anything he didn't want. She never had been capable of that. No one was.

"We're going to talk. Instead of futile attempts on the phone, I decided to come in person," he said. "If I had known about your grandmother, I would have waited. We can either talk now or in a day or two. But since we're both here, I'm not leaving until we get some things settled."

"Everything was settled years ago. Seems to me, anyway." She knew she sounded petulant, but she couldn't help it. Seeing him brought all the memories to the forefront. She didn't like it, she should be over him!

Instead she felt drawn to the man. Just being near him excited her senses, made her aware of her own femininity. She wanted to rail at him for leaving her. She wanted to discover what he'd been doing for the last five years. How she wished she could change the past!

"Running away never solved anything, Margot," he said.

"Maybe Georgia and I should wait in the living room," Shelby said.

"No need. I have nothing to discuss with Rand. Sorry you made the trip for nothing." Margot turned and almost ran up the stairs, escape uppermost in her mind. So what if he thought she was running away. It was too late to dream dreams with Rand at the center.

Truth be told, she'd been operating on sheer nervous energy for days and she'd explode if she didn't get away. This was too much. First her grandmother's illness; then her unexpected death; now Rand's reappearance after hearing nothing from him for five years!

It felt as if the world was crashing down on her. She could use a little help, not have more problems thrown her way. Would she be capable of administering the probate and managing the estate until the inheritance was settled? How could she cope with the myriad problems if her whole being became caught up in the old fascination, or the endless recriminations and regrets tied with Rand?

The man she'd loved more than life itself.

The man who had abandoned her, betraying her faith at the worst moment in her life. First she'd lost their unborn baby, then her husband.

The man she sometimes feared she still loved despite all that had passed between them.

No, no, no, she murmured as she hurried down the long hallway.

She refused to let herself be caught up with that reckless emotion of love. It hurt too much when it ended. Picking up the pieces of her shattered life had not been easy. But she'd managed. So what if she didn't experience the joyful delights she'd found with Rand. Neither did she have the depths of bitter pain and betrayal to contend with, either.

Except with the startling revelation from her grandmother just before she'd died.

It couldn't be true, could it? Even Harriet Beaufort couldn't have been that self-serving, that vindictive, that manipulative. That strange tale had been the ramblings of a delirious, dying woman, that's all, Margot tried to convince herself. Nothing more.

She closed her bedroom door and flung herself on her bed. The room was dim. Out of habit, she'd closed the drapes earlier to keep the hot sun from fading the carpet. Now she wrapped herself in the light coverlet and closed her eyes. Fatigue gripped her. She longed for the oblivion of sleep, but Rand's face danced before her eyes.

Why had he come?

*   *   *

Rand watched Margot flee up the stairs. For a moment he almost pursued her, fed up with her refusal to talk with him. Nothing had changed. She avoided him at every turn. Just as she had so long ago. Only this time he would not be put off.

His attorneys could have had the papers delivered. His own curiosity and need for closure had him determined to deliver the papers in person. Only he hadn't expected Harriet's death. For a moment he wondered what Margot would do without her formidable grandmother to hide behind.

"Come in and sit down, Rand," Shelby said, looking after her sister with worry in her eyes. "I'm sure she'll be back soon. It's been a stressful few days."

"Longer than that for Margot," Georgia said. "She's the one who cared for Grandmother while she was ill."

"Was Harriet sick for long?"

"No, only a few weeks," Georgia said. "But it's still taken its toll. She looks exhausted." She turned toward the living room. "Tell us what you've been doing, Rand. I haven't seen you in years."

"It has been a while," Rand acknowledged as he followed the two sisters into the huge formal living room. Quickly he noted the elegant furnishings, the paintings by the old masters on the wall. Nothing had altered since he'd last been in this room. It still felt as cold and impersonal as a hotel lobby, or a museum recreation. It was a perfect setting for Harriet Beaufort.

Natchez, Mississippi, was full of antebellum homes. Many of them were in various state of disrepair, or had been turned over to an historical trust. Only a few of the old mansions were still owned privately. Harriet Beaufort had gripped hers with both hands, tightly, changing nothing in the home that had been in her husband's family for generations. She had taken inordinate pride in every stick of furniture, every painting, every piece of silver.

He'd once longed for such a setting—discovering that it offered only cold comfort once he attained it.

While the house remained the same, Margot's younger sisters had changed. Shelby was striking, tall and slender and lovely. She'd been nineteen when he last saw her. Still living under Harriet Beaufort's domineering thumb, shy and studious. He wondered what she was doing now. Did the sisters all still live in the old family home? Or had they, like Margot at that age, broken away and tried to make a life away from Beaufort Hall?

Georgia offered him some punch from the silver bowl on the buffet against the wall and sat beside him on the brocade sofa. She'd changed the most, he mused, sipping the small glass she'd brought. A high school senior when his marriage ended, she'd blossomed into a beautiful woman, bright and sassy if the trend of her conversation was any indication. Had she stopped talking since they'd sat down?

"—so of course I had to come home, just like you, Rand. Family rallies around in the time of crisis, right? It wasn't easy getting time off. We are always swamped. But then, hospitals are always shorthanded and the number of patients seems to increase every year."

"Georgia, you're babbling. Shut up and let Rand get a word in edgewise," Shelby said, sitting on the chair near the sofa. She didn't appear as friendly as her younger sister, Rand noted. From loyalty to Margot? Or her own innate shyness?

"I'm interested in what she has to say," he replied. It paid to discover all he could about the people he would be dealing with. His years in business had proved that. These women had the closest ties to Margot. He would learn more about her through them.

"Do you both still live here?" he asked.

Shelby shook her head. "Actually Georgia

and I live in New Orleans. We have for several years.''

"Moved out as soon as we were old enough to escape," Georgia said irrepressibly.

He raised an eyebrow in surprise. ''You've been in New Orleans all this time? You should have called me.''

Shelby looked at him gravely. ''I didn't think you wanted any more involvement with the Beauforts,'' she said. ''And it's not as if we move in the same circles, is it?''

''As Georgia says, we're family.'' Until he got Margot's signature on the papers he carried—until the final link was severed.

Of course he had not thought about family ties when Margot had left. Angry at her defection, he'd been determined to prove to the world, and to himself, that he needed no one. His parents had never understood. The new family he tried to forge had come to a tragic end; going alone had been the only option he'd considered.

Georgia took a sip of punch and studied Rand. ''We missed you,'' she said.

If he were honest, he'd admit to missing them. Missing Margot most of all, but also her adoring sisters. He'd been an only child. He'd enjoyed watching the sisters interact during the short months of his marriage. Had been almost envious of their closeness.

"Where do you two live?"

"I live near St. Charles Street, in a great apartment not far from the downtown area. Georgia has a place in Metairie. She works at St. Joseph's Hospital," Shelby replied.

"And Margot?" He had to ask. Curiosity, a burning desire to know more about her even as he was about to cut her totally from his life, surprised him.

"She has an apartment here in Natchez. I don't think she ever goes to New Orleans. She never comes to visit us," Georgia said.

The sudden silence proved awkward. Each knew why Margot never returned to New Orleans, though no one said it aloud. The memories were too painful.

"You're planning to stay, aren't you?" Georgia asked to break the tension. "There are a dozen bedrooms here. And it would be so nice to have you right on the spot to help out. Being in business you must have a better idea of what to expect and how to handle things than we do—we don't have a clue. And I hate the thought of Margot coping with it all on her own—look how thin she is, and how tired she seems. Since she is the eldest, Grandmother designated her as executrix. Now I'm worried about her.''

''I hadn't really planned to stay that long,'' Rand said, setting his glass on a coaster on the Queen Anne table. From the dirty glasses, cups and plates stacked haphazardly here and there, he guessed the wake had ended only a short time before he arrived. Thank goodness he'd been late enough to miss that!

''Oh, please. It'll be days or weeks before the estate gets put into probate and then months for it to go through the entire process. Margot will probably have a dozen questions. We've never gone through this before,'' Georgia said, leaning close, her eyes beseeching.

''If you can manage it, Rand, please, do spare a few days at least. Just to make sure Margot has a handle on things. I can only be here until tomorrow. I hate the thought of leaving Margot alone to deal with all this, but I can't get any more time off from work right now. I'll come back soon for another short visit. But it would mean a lot to know she has someone with her,'' Shelby added.

''I have to be back on duty tomorrow night. Shelby and I are driving back together. Do stay, Rand,'' Georgia urged.

''I hardly think Margot would appreciate the arrangement.''

Surprised, he actually considered it. Primarily to see the expression on Margot's face when she heard.

Darkness and silence filled the bedroom when Margot awoke. Flicking on her bedside lamp, she looked at the clock. It was after eight. Slowly she stretched, still feeling tired, over-whelmed. Life had been simpler two months ago, before her grandmother had become so ill, before Margot's world had been turned upside down a second time.

Changing from her black dress to a light robe, Margot fastened the buttons pensively. She was starving—not surprising when she considered how little she'd eaten recently. Had Rand left already?

Hurrying down the stairs, she listened for voices. Where were Shelby and Georgia? The rooms were empty. The living room tidy once again. Obviously they'd cleaned up the mess. Had they gone out to dinner?

Pushing open the door into the kitchen, Margot stopped in surprise. Rand looked up from the open refrigerator and caught her eye, letting his gaze travel over the robe. A gleam of predatory male interest suddenly shone in his eyes. He straightened slowly and closed the door.

"I thought you would have been long gone by now," Margot said. For one awful moment, she wished she'd brushed her hair, freshened her makeup. Pushing the thought aside, she tried to figure out why he was still here. And how to slow the rapid increase in her heart rate. She would not let herself be attracted to the man, just because he looked wonderful, tanned and fit. Ruthlessly ignoring the clamoring of her senses, she tried to remain cool.

"Not yet. Your sisters are changing their clothes, then we're planning on dinner. I thought I'd look around and see what we might find to eat in here. Otherwise, we'll go out. What happened to your grandmother's cook?"

"I gave her the week off. She was quite upset. She was devoted to Harriet."

"Mmm." He leaned against the counter, crossing his arms over his chest. Margot noticed he'd discarded his suit jacket somewhere along the way. His tie was loosened at the neck, the collar button unfastened. He'd rolled up his sleeves over muscular arms. He looked at ease, at home. And fascinating. She remembered being held in those strong arms. Being kissed—

She looked away, trying to forget the stubborn memories.

"Some people liked my grandmother," she

said defensively, hearing the skepticism in his tone. Rand had never been one of them.

"Hungry?" he asked, deliberately changing the subject.

Margot hesitated. While she didn't mind hunting up some soup or sandwich fixings, she hadn't expected to share a meal with Rand. And especially not cook him one. On the other hand, if he took her sisters to dinner, she'd spend tonight alone. She didn't want to miss the evening with Georgia and Shelby—their time together was too short as it was.

"Margot, it's a straightforward question. Are you hungry? You look as if you're considering some major life change," he said impatiently.

"I already had that." The words came unbidden. Horrified, she stared at him in dismay.

He drew a deep breath. "That's what I've come to discuss."

Shaking her head, Margot stepped back against the swinging door. "No. Not now. It's far too late to change anything by talk, Rand. If you and my sisters want, I can prepare something for dinner."

"Or we could order something, have it delivered."

"Oops," Georgia said as she pushed against the door and barged into Margot. Peering around the corner, she stepped into the kitchen once her sister moved.

"I see you're up. Hungry? We thought we'd go out for dinner, unless you found something, Rand?"

"Nothing that wouldn't take a long time to prepare. I was telling Margot that we could order in."

"Oh, that's sounds great. Does that Chinese place on Royal Street still deliver?" Georgia asked Margot.

"Yes, I get food from there all the time."

"Too busy to cook?" Rand asked.

She shook her head. "I just don't like to cook for one," she replied. If she didn't look directly at him, maybe she could ignore him, ignore the emotions that were all mixed up. Maybe she could pretend he was just an acquaintance. Letting Georgia carry the conversation, Margot tried to concentrate, but her thoughts were churning too much to pay strict attention.

Until Georgia said something she couldn't possibly believe.

"What did you say?" Margot asked, her startled eyes meeting her sister's.

Georgia looked at her, smiling brightly. "Just that Shelby and I are pleased Rand has agreed to stay to help you during the next few days. We feel terrible leaving you with all the work.

And we didn't like the thought of your remaining here all alone.''

Horrified, Margot turned to look at Rand.

His gaze met hers and her heart sank. The unholy gleam in his eye did not auger well for the future.

CHAPTER TWO

MARGOT stared at him in disbelief. "You are *not* staying!"

"He can help," Georgia said.

"We don't need help. Not his kind in any event," Margot protested.

Rand stared at her, trying to ignore the clamor of his senses, the heightened awareness being near her engendered. Even with her hair mussed and dark circles beneath her eyes, she was beautiful. Too thin, yet with an allure that still had the power to captivate. He instantly evaluated his options. He could find his jacket, pull out the papers and insist she sign them. Take that final step to end their marriage for once and all. That would remove him from her proximity.

Or he could stay. Have it out with her, let her know how her leaving had affected him over the years. Tell her how disgusted he'd been when she'd chosen her grandmother's home over theirs.

But something held him back. She looked too

frail, too fragile, too on edge—as if she were at the end of her rope. For all he knew she'd be glad to sign, glad to get him out of her life. She'd made her position clear years ago. Yet something still held back the words. He hadn't succeeded by ignoring his instincts.

"I've already told you I intend to stay a couple of days. If you don't need my help with the estate, then I'll be gone—*after* we have our talk." And after she signed those papers.

Margot stared at him mutinously, her eyes flashing fire. She brushed a hand through her hair. Rand clenched one hand to keep from reaching out to touch that silky mane. His fingertips remembered the soft texture. Did it still smell of lilacs? Taking a deep breath, he imagined he could detect the scent from where he stood.

Margot raised her chin, her eyes still angry. He almost smiled at the familiar gesture as bittersweet memories surfaced.

"The time for us to talk was five years ago. There's nothing left to say. But if you don't mind wasting your time hanging around here, do what you want."

"I don't think it'll be a waste of time," Rand said as he studied her through narrowed eyes. "If nothing else, we'll clear things up between us. But after Georgia and Shelby leave. I do not plan to air our dirty laundry before all and sundry.''

''Since you're here for dinner, I'll go change.''

Leaving the kitchen with her head held high, Margot hurried to change into casual clothes. She wondered if she could get Rand alone tonight and find out what he had to say. What was there to say that would make any difference? The past couldn't be altered.

Shelby and Georgia were chatting easily with Rand when Margot entered the living room a few minutes later.

''We ordered Chinese,'' Shelby said. ''It'll be here soon. Want something to drink?''

Margot motioned Shelby to stay seated. ''I'll get some iced tea.'' A quick glance at Rand showed him firmly ensconced in the chair near the sofa, his long legs stretched out before him, his right hand casually holding a tall glass. For a moment her heart threatened to stop, then skipped a beat and began to pound. When he looked at her with those dark eyes, she felt the heat rise in her cheeks. One look and she spun back to that shy college freshman who had been so enamored with the young businessman who had singled her out and courted her so assiduously. Of course, he wasn't that much older than she, only five years. He'd been twenty-five when they married. He was just thirty-one now. But when he'd been courting, he'd seemed so much more mature than she felt.

Turning away she knew she had to get control of her emotions. She had to ignore the pull of attraction that rose despite her best efforts at keeping a distance. Rand was not for her. He'd proven that five years ago.

"Rand has been telling us about his plans for expanding his shipping line," Shelby said. "I told him I worked for an insurance company that handles a lot of marine accounts. Maybe he'll throw some business our way."

Margot sat gingerly on a chair opposite Rand, hoping her sisters wouldn't comment on how far the seat was from the rest of them.

"*Your* shipping line?" she asked.

Nodding, Rand replied, "I bought enough shares from Stemple to gain controlling interest."

She studied her glass of tea, wondering if she dare ask how he'd done that. He'd often talked of his plans for moving up in the shipping line, for making it big when they'd first married. She wasn't surprised to learn he'd succeeded. But he must have risked a lot to achieve so much in only five years. Would a show of curiosity on her part be misconstrued as interest? Would he read more into a casual inquiry than was warranted? She couldn't seem to help being curious. She had often thought about him over the years; ached for his arms around her, longed to hear his voice.

What else had he been doing since she'd last seen him? Or had business consumed him to the exclusion of anything else?

He'd worked incessantly in the weeks before she left, to the exclusion of everything else. She wondered if he still worked nonstop, forgetting about people and other commitments in his quest to make more money, to get ahead and become rich and powerful. Did he still strive for that goal, or had things changed at all in his life since she left?

"How long did you say it would be before the food arrives?" she asked. She refused to be drawn into his life again. Once had been enough.

Rand's teeth gleamed white against his tan as he smiled directly at her. "Changing the subject, Margot, or just trying to ignore that I'm here?"

She glared at him. "That's hard to do when you take up so much space."

He raised an eyebrow sardonically. "One small chair?"

He seemed to dominate the room. She could feel his presence where she sat. A quick glance at her sisters surprised her. Didn't they feel that magnetism, the power? Was she alone affected?

Time dragged. When the food finally arrived, Margot insisted they eat in the dining room, though her sisters had opted for the more informal kitchen. But Margot didn't want informality or a semblance of coziness with Rand. She needed to keep him at a distance to keep her own sanity.

Even with the length of the table between them, however, she was aware of his every move. Of how he cut his egg roll. Of the way his throat moved when he swallowed, the way his hands held the teacup, the way his hot gaze focused on her more often than she wanted.

The meal seemed endless, and Margot thought she would go crazy.

When they finished, Georgia and Shelby insisted on doing the few dishes they'd used.

Margot faced Rand. "We could talk now," she said, certain she wouldn't sleep a wink if she didn't discover why he'd come.

"Not tonight, Margot. You look exhausted. Why not get a good night's sleep first?" Rand said gently.

Great—he thought she looked awful. Not the words a woman wanted to hear. Especially from a man she'd like to show she'd managed fine without.

Georgia popped back into the dining room and wiped up the table. "Am I interrupting?"

Margot shook her head and rose. "Not at all." She would have argued with Rand, but he was right, she was too tired.

"I'm going up to bed."

"Good idea," Rand said, his dark eyes mocking.

"Are you all right?" Georgia asked.

"I'll be fine once I get some rest." And once she got away from Rand. She prayed Harriet's estate would be clear-cut and easy to deal with. If there was no need for Rand's help, he could leave tomorrow when her sisters left. After they had that talk.

That would give her time alone to close up the house and search through her grandmother's papers to see if she could discover anything surrounding her father's disappearance.

"Then I'll see you in the morning," Rand said. "Sleep well."

She wanted to throw back a scathing comment, but wouldn't give him the satisfaction. Nor raise any doubts in Georgia's mind.

As Margot prepared for bed, she forced her thoughts away from her husband and tried to remember as much as she could about her father. He'd married her mother for her money and when it wasn't forthcoming, he left. That is, if the teachings of a lifetime could be believed. But Harriet Beaufort's delirious words during her final weeks raised strong doubts in Margot's mind.

Margot had grown up believing her father deserted her mother, broke her heart and caused her death. That he had turned his back on his children, his responsibilities, and had taken off for greener pastures. Maybe, like Rand, his wife and family hadn't been enough to hold him.

But was that the whole story? Was it even the *truth*?

Rand watched Margot leave, a common occurrence around her, he thought wryly. Wanting some time alone, he let himself out onto the wide veranda. The sultry night air felt good after the sterile coolness inside the house.

He walked to the edge and gazed over the dark lawn. He'd have to call the office first thing tomorrow and inform his secretary he wouldn't be coming in. After Margot's sisters left, they could talk.

He had wanted to see her again. Irrational, he knew. And lately everything had a logic that made for no wasted emotion, no wrong moves. For five years he'd tried to put her out of his mind. Sometimes even succeeding for a few weeks at a time.

Then he'd see someone who reminded him of her. Or catch a hint of the perfume she used to wear, or hear a song she loved. Defying logic, memories would flood to the surface. Sometimes he'd dream about her. It was past time to cut the tie, get her out of his life and move on.

Yet seeing her caused many of the familiar feelings to resurface. What was there about Margot that lingered? That caused a ruthless, logical businessman to postpone a confrontation and stay when she so clearly didn't want him?

Margot slept in late the next morning. She looked for her sisters after she dressed. They were in the kitchen already preparing lunch. Feeling extraneous, she leaned against the counter and chatted desultorily while Shelby prepared a shrimp salad, a fruit salad and cold cuts.

Georgia set the table and called Rand.

Scarcely greeting Rand, Margot sat and wished for an appetite.

Shelby looked at Georgia and Margot, and spoke, "Margot, I'm sorry to leave you with all the work regarding the estate, but if it makes it any easier, I for one never plan to live in this house and vote we sell it."

Surprised, Rand looked at Margot. "I thought

this was your family home. Hasn't it been in your family for generations?''

She nodded.

"Do you want to sell?" he asked.

For a moment Margot thought about it. She hadn't looked beyond discovering what she could about her father's disappearance. Shelby's idea had merit.

"Might as well. I don't want to live here." There were no happy memories, only those of a bitter old woman who demanded prestige and power and money and didn't care who she stepped on to get it.

"Me, neither," Georgia said firmly. "I couldn't wait to escape when I graduated from high school. Sell the blasted thing. We can split the money and each buy something more suitable for our current life-styles. I love New Orleans. With my share from the sale, maybe I could buy a condo or something."

"We'd need to go through the furnishings and things, keep what we want, and get rid of the rest," Margot said slowly, already dreading the monumental task of sorting through several generations of accumulated furnishings, clothes and memorabilia before they could put the place up for sale.

"Goodness, what an undertaking. I'll try to come over on weekends," Shelby said.

"I can come up on my days off," Georgia added.

Margot nodded. "I've been away from the shop so long a couple more weeks won't hurt. Jessie can keep it going a little longer on her own. I'll start and y'all come and help when you can."

Georgia and Shelby looked at Rand. "Maybe you could lend a hand," Georgia said brightly.

Rand nodded, his gaze fixed on Margot. "I'll stay for a couple of days, as I said I would."

"You don't have to stay at all!" she snapped.

Rand smiled, almost enjoying her frustration. He'd stay another day or two, if only to watch her move in the rarefied air she'd been born into—and get her out of his system once and for all.

Shelby and Georgia planned to leave shortly after lunch. Once packed, Shelby sought Margot. She found her sister in the study going through some of the papers on the desk.

"Are you feeling all right?" she asked, closing the door softly behind her. Crossing to sit on the edge of the desk, she looked closely at her sister.

"I'm tired, that's all. It's been an exhausting few weeks. And Rand's unexpected reappearance hasn't helped. I'll be fine in a day or two."

"Rand looks good," Shelby said, playing with the letter opener.

"No matchmaking," Margot warned. "I won't be drawn in again."

Shelby shrugged and glanced around the room. "It was a long time ago, sis. People change. Men never say much, but maybe he came because he wants another chance."

"I doubt it." But for an instant a flicker of hope glimmered. Could that be the reason for Rand's visit?

"Why else would he show up?"

"I have no idea...he's scarcely said two words to me."

"Give him a break. He hasn't had a moment alone with you since he arrived."

Margot kept silent. She wondered why Rand had really come. Was he trying to make amends? Had he changed?

It didn't matter. The chasm was too large. If she couldn't depend on her husband in a time of crisis, she'd rather go it alone.

"He'll be gone in a day or so and things will return to normal," Margot said sadly. Closing her eyes, she wondered if she would ever regain her strength, ever feel full of energy again.

"It's odd to know Grandmother's gone. She was such a strong force in our lives," Shelby said, idly tracing patterns with the letter opener.

"Too strong," Margot said. "She wasn't happy unless she could run things—even our lives. She practically forced me to date that friend of hers, Philip Grant, and he's years older than I. She kept harping on what a wonderful alliance that would be."

"Is that why you never divorced—to make sure you couldn't be persuaded into an alliance?" Shelby asked unexpectedly, looking directly at Margot.

"Alliance. Isn't that dynastic? I never thought about it before, but do you suppose that's what she and grandfather had—an alliance instead of a rich and happy marriage?" Margot asked, deliberately sidestepping her sister's personal question. Was that the reason Rand had come, to discuss a divorce? Her heart lurched, began to beat heavily. She wasn't ready for such a decision.

"I don't know, she sure was taken with the Beaufort family. It always seemed as if she thought it deserves some kind of monument or something. And she just married into it. It wasn't as if she'd been born into the family. She wasn't really a Beaufort."

Margot looked at her sister. "We aren't really Beauforts, either, you know."

Shelby looked puzzled for a moment. "Oh,

yes, you're right in a way. I had almost forgotten.''

"Harriet was Mama's mother. But when Mama married our father, she would have taken his last name. She obviously took the Beaufort name back after the divorce and changed ours to match.''

"Because she was so angry at our father, she didn't want us to use his name, do you suppose?''

Margot shrugged, longing to tell her sister what Harriet had said. Suddenly she had more questions than she could count. What had happened twenty-three years ago? Had their father really abandoned them as they'd always been told? And where was he now?

Margot saw her sisters off, remaining on the veranda after the taillights disappeared down the long driveway. Even in the shade, the afternoon felt oppressive. Conscious of Rand standing a few feet away, watching her, she shivered despite the heat and crossed her arms across her chest. If he didn't stop, he'd drive her crazy!

Taking a deep breath, she turned and looked at him, tilting her chin, drawing on years of training under the eagle eye of her grandmother.

"You can leave now as well," she said politely, the edge of frustration coloring her tone.

Slowly he smiled, amusement dancing in his eyes as he stood leaning against one of the support pillars, his arms across his broad chest, his suit jacket once again discarded, his shirtsleeves rolled up. He had to be warm in the late-afternoon sun, but he looked cool and controlled.

"I don't think so, Margot. We have some unfinished business between us and now is as good a time to get it resolved as any, wouldn't you say?"

"Is that why you came? To talk about the past?"

"Why I came isn't as important as why I'm staying."

"And why is that?"

"I told you, to get things resolved."

"Seems to me we resolved things five years ago."

"Really?" He stepped forward, his arms dropping to his sides. "And I said running away never solved anything. Did you ever think about me after you left, Margot?"

Before she could even think of a response, he lowered his head and covered her mouth with his.

Shocked, Margot felt the past and present merge until she had no idea where she was. Rand's lips moved against hers as passionately as ever, as familiar as her own heartbeat. For a long moment the world stood still. Every cell in Margot's body recognized Rand's touch, his taste, his scent. His fingers threaded into her hair as he cradled her head in his strong hands. The world spun and Margot almost forgot the years that had separated them. Almost forgot the painful past and the tragedy that had ripped their world apart.

She couldn't think, couldn't remember, could only feel. Feel the spiraling sensations that danced throughout her. Feel the glorious heat that warmed her soul. Feel the past and present swirl together until there was only the timeless call of passion.

Endless eons later, Rand raised his face, his eyes narrowed as he took in her bemused expression. When his features hardened, she drew back, realizing instantly what she'd allowed. What she'd participated in. What she'd enjoyed.

"I didn't leave you, Rand. I left an empty apartment." She bit out the words, and whirled, walking swiftly toward the front door. Confusion gripped her. How could she have responded so fervently? She should have pulled back at the first sign he wanted to kiss her. But she hadn't expected it.

And once he touched her she'd been lost.

He swung around and called after her, "You

don't have your grandmother to run to this time, Margot. There's just you and me here now.''

She paused by the door and stiffened. "And pretty soon there'll only be me, Rand. You won't stay. I don't seem to have much luck with men staying in my life, do I?''

"What men?'' His voice was sharp.

She turned to look at him. "First my father, then you. Isn't that enough?''

"If you are comparing me to your father, maybe you should also compare yourself with your mother. What part did she play in driving him away?''

"What do you mean?''

"I still remember your telling me how you felt by his abandoning you and your sisters when you were a child. But maybe part of the fault lay with your mother. Maybe you and I were only repeating history—maybe she left him.''

"Actually,'' Margot began slowly, the urge to share her discovery too strong to resist. "I'm not sure he did leave. Voluntarily, that is.''

"What do you mean?''

She hesitated. "I guess it can't hurt to tell you.'' She gazed over the wide expanse of lawn. "Something my grandmother said just before she died makes me wonder if my father left of his own volition, or was driven away. She made it sound as if she had something to do with his leaving. She forced him to go."

"How could he have been driven away by Harriet?"

"I don't know. That's what I plan to find out. All my life I've thought it was something I did that made him leave. Maybe he didn't want little girls, what if he wanted sons instead. Or maybe I was too bratty."

"For heaven's sake, you were three when he left. You couldn't have done anything."

She nodded. "Rationally, as an adult, I know that. I think I know that. But we're talking about a child growing up. My mother was dead, my father gone. Kids take on responsibility when there is none there. He could have left because of me, because he didn't want to be tied down with a child."

"Highly unlikely. If he hadn't wanted a child, they would have stopped at one, not had two more—although if you were only three at the time, I assume he wouldn't even have known about your mother being pregnant with Georgia."

She shrugged. "I don't know much about it, but I plan to find out. If there is anything in Grandmother's papers, I'll find it."

"What are you expecting, some sort of jour-

nal in which she confesses all?'' he asked scathingly.

Margot lifted her chin. ''That's unlikely, I
know. Yet there might be something somewhere. It doesn't have to be an easy task. It
would make a world of difference to me to find
out he hadn't deliberately abandoned me—us.''

''What do Shelby and Georgia think about
this?''

''I didn't tell them. There's the possibility
that Harriet was merely delirious and didn't
know what she was saying. Maybe she was hal-
lucinating. I don't know. The first time she said
she'd fixed it so he had to leave, I really thought
that's what it was. But she repeated it over and
over, and I began to think maybe it wasn't just
rambling, but the past coming alive for her.''

''And if you don't find anything?'' he asked.

''If I can't find anything in her papers, I'll
look farther afield, see if anyone in town remembers that far back.''

''You should hire a private detective to find
out.''

She shook her head, smiling in embarrassment. ''It's not that big a deal. I don't need to
find the man, just discover if he left because he
didn't want his daughters, or if Harriet drove
him away. It's been twenty-three years. If he
hasn't tried to contact us after all this time, I

guess he doesn't want to see me or my sisters. But I would like to know.''

"It won't change things. He'll still be gone.''

"It could change how I feel about him,'' she said slowly. "All my life I've felt abandoned. Maybe I wasn't.''

He had no concept of feeling abandoned or feeling as if he were the cause. Except by Margot's departure. He was not here to become involved in Margot's troubles. He'd come to end the connection. But she looked so alone by the door, so confused. Once he told her why he'd come, he'd have to leave.

But he didn't need to tell her tonight.

"You realize it is probably a futile effort?'' he asked.

She nodded.

Against all logic, he spoke, "I'll help you look, as long as I'm here.''

Rand wondered why he kept postponing his departure. It had nothing to do with how she felt when he kissed her. Nothing to do with the passion he felt in her. He wasn't even sure why he'd given in to impulse and kissed her, except she'd been standing there and he hadn't been able to resist.

It changed nothing.

They'd had seven glorious months together.

When their happiness ended with her miscarriage, she'd packed and left.

He wouldn't leave himself open to such desolation again. Once he obtained the divorce, he had no immediate plans to remarry. In the morning, he'd give her the papers.

Or, he could stay through the weekend. Today was Thursday, it would only be three more days before he had to be back at work on Monday. He could stay and help Margot look through her grandmother's papers to see if the old woman had indeed been instrumental in driving away her father. Stay and prove to himself that he was over her.

"Why would she do such a thing?" he asked a minute later, considering the different ramifications.

"I don't know. I know she wanted my mother to marry into an old Mississippi family. Instead she ran off with my father. They settled here at Grandmother's insistence, I think." Margot refused to give voice to the hurtful words her grandmother always said, calling her father a no-good, worthless drifter. A child didn't need to hear that about her own father. But her grandmother had not been big on psychology for children and forged her own ruthless path.

"Let's get started," he said, heading for the door.

Surprised, Margot looked at him. "I thought you wanted to talk."

"Later."

"I don't want you to stay," she said desperately as he stepped closer.

"And I didn't want you to leave five years ago. Looks like we don't always get what we want. Where do you want to start with Harriet's papers?"

Margot flung open the door and hastened through before Rand could get too close. Why had he agreed to help her? Distrustful, she glanced at him, keeping her distance.

"I'll take the help," she said carefully, "but no more kisses." She didn't care if she gave herself away, it was too dangerous to have him think he could kiss her whenever he wanted. She wasn't sure she could withstand temptation.

He smiled sardonically and deliberately took a threatening step closer. "No promises, Margot. For someone who says she doesn't want any more kisses, you sure responded as if you did."

"I don't want to discuss it!"

"Running away again?" he asked softly.

She shook her head and walked calmly through the foyer to a door at the far end, her heart racing. She would never admit it, but running seemed the most prudent plan right now!

"Harriet used this as her study and office. Any papers she had would be in here."

Rand stepped into the doorway and looked around. "Shouldn't take too long to go through this." There was a small desk, one old oak file cabinet and several shelves of books. "However, I doubt you'll find anything from twenty years ago here. There's not enough room to store records for that many years. Would she have put earlier years elsewhere?" he asked.

"In the attic, I suppose. It covers the entire width of the house. We were never allowed up there to play when we were children. I don't think I've been up there more than a half-dozen times in my whole life."

"Interesting possibility. Let's eliminate this first, then we'll check that out."

Margot glanced at her watch. "It'll be dinnertime soon. Caroline isn't due back until tomorrow. Want me to fix us sandwiches or something?"

"We could order in a pizza," he said, already opening the top drawer of the polished desk. He missed the look on Margot's face.

For a moment another time flashed before her eyes. Ordering pizza had been their one extravagance when they'd been married. One they indulged in as frequently as their budget would allow. Memories bubbled up, splashed over. She hugged herself and looked around. She hadn't had a pizza in years.

Yet it obviously meant nothing to Rand. Unaware he'd said anything disturbing, he withdrew a stack of papers and began to sort them. Shaking off her melancholy, Margot went to the phone and dialed. She had to put things into perspective. They were married, yet had lived apart for far longer than they'd lived together. They had their own lives now. And no room for memories of their time together.

In fact, she was somewhat surprised Rand had never filed for divorce. She knew why she hadn't, but why hadn't he? She opened her mouth to ask him, and snapped it shut. Her life was in enough turmoil right now, the last thing she needed was further discussion on why their marriage had ended. And when to finalize the demise. Maybe once she learned about her father, she could move on. And if that meant legally ending their marriage, she'd consider it.

But what if Rand didn't want to end it, a small voice whispered. What if he had hopes she'd return? What if his kiss had been to prove to her they still belonged together?

Nonsense! It was time to forget the past, and concentrate on the future—and if she could discover the truth about her father. Not the truth about Rand.

Yet why had that thought crept up? Wasn't she sure she knew the truth? When she had needed him most after losing the baby, he'd been conspicuously missing. She had left, and he hadn't even tried to contact her, hadn't followed to bring her home. If he'd cared at all, he would have at least phoned her.

"Pizza will be here in a half hour. What are you doing?" she said, placing the phone receiver back in its cradle.

"I'm sorting business papers from personal correspondence, or anything that looks like it might be personal," he said, not even looking up.

Margot pulled a drawer from the desk and took it to a chair, sitting with it on her lap. Soon only the sound of ruffling paper filled the air.

Once she had an idea how long it would take to clear out the house, she could prepare for the sale. In a few weeks, a couple of months at the most, the albatross would be gone and she would have nothing tying her to Natchez—except her fledgling business.

For a moment she wondered if she should consider moving to New Orleans to be near Georgia and Shelby. But the familiar ache vetoed that idea. She wasn't sure she'd ever want to return to the Crescent City. New Orleans was where Rand lived—where they'd lived together. And where their unborn baby had died. The memories were too painful. There were just some things she couldn't do.

When the pizza arrived, Margot brought the box, plates and napkins into the study. Rand stood, scooped up two pieces, and headed for the door. "I'll be back," he said cryptically, and kept walking.

Margot nibbled at a slice, wondering where he'd gone. She heard his car, then silence.

At least it made eating easier. She was too aware of the man whenever he was near. Too aware of the potent feelings that continued to dance along her nerve endings. She should be focusing on her quest, searching for an answer. Instead she had watched Rand as he quickly scanned papers and placed them in different piles. His dark hair had fallen across his brow in disarray as he'd run his fingers through it in the course of the afternoon. She'd longed to brush it back, ask him what he'd been doing for the last five years.

And to ask if he ever thought about her.

CHAPTER THREE

DAYDREAMS aren't worth the paper they're written on, Harriet had often said. Margot could hear her grandmother's voice echoing on the night breeze. And daydreams about Rand sweeping her off her feet and demanding that she return to him were as worthless as any. She must still be tired to permit such foolishness, Margot thought.

It was fully dark by the time Rand turned into the driveway. Margot watched from her wicker rocking chair on the veranda. The temperature had dropped a few degrees with the setting sun. A light breeze blew from the river, cooling things even more. She had skimmed as many papers as she could find in the study until her eyes had become bleary. Seeking solace, she'd come to sit in the dark, on the veranda where she could smell the lingering scent of sweet olive, and hear the gentle murmur from the Mississippi River. And allow her imagination free rein—just this once.

She watched as Rand pulled up before the

house and got out, reaching back inside the car for numerous bags and packages and a slim briefcase. He started for the door. Margot knew the moment he saw her—he was almost even with her.

"I wondered if you'd left," she said. The word *again* hovered unspoken.

He walked over and sank down on a matching rocker beside her, placing the bags on the veranda.

"I didn't come prepared to stay. I had one clean shirt in the car, but if we're going to be plowing through dusty boxes in your attic, I wanted something more casual than an Armani suit."

She nodded, noting the quiet pride when he mentioned his suit. He'd succeeded, just as he'd always wanted. Did it make him happy? she wondered. Did he ever think about what they had started building together—a family?

Did you ever think about me after you left? he'd asked.

She could have answered his question. She had thought about him endlessly when she'd first returned home. Expected him to come and get her, to demand she return to their home, to insist her place was with him, that he couldn't live without her. She'd expected him to prove to her that he loved her far more than business.

And once the initial hurt had faded, they could have built a future together.

But there had been nothing. No calls, no letters, no visits. She suspected that he'd been secretly relieved to be able to discard his wife so easily. Didn't men want children—a son? And she hadn't been able to provide that.

"I'm sorry," she said in a low voice, the old pain surging to the forefront.

"For what? I volunteered to stay. At least through the weekend."

"For losing our baby," she whispered. "I know you blamed me."

"What?" He sounded shocked. "Margot, I never blamed you for losing the baby."

"It's all right, you know. I blame myself," she said.

"No. Miscarriages happen. If anything—I blamed myself. If we hadn't had to live in that apartment where you had to walk up two flights of stairs every day, maybe you wouldn't have lost the baby. If I'd been any kind of husband, I could have provided better for you, for the baby."

"Don't say that. It's not true. Exercise is good for pregnant women. It wasn't your fault." Margot was stunned at Rand's words. *He had blamed himself?*

"It sure felt as if it were at the time. But as

the years have passed, I wonder if there is any fault? Things like that happen. They're tragic, but not always avoidable. Can you look at any one thing and say it caused the miscarriage?''

She shook her head, blinking against sudden tears. She was through crying. She'd cried a river's worth over the years. Yet the old pain never went completely away. She would always long for her precious baby.

But with his admission that he'd also blamed himself, that he didn't hold her totally responsible, some of her guilt eased. Maybe it was the way things were meant to be. She'd loved him deeply, longed to have his children, to build a loving and happy family with Rand. And failed.

She looked over. He was hard to see in the darkness. His silhouette stood out against the soft illumination spilling from the windows. Her heart skipped a beat and began to pound. Surreptitiously rubbing her damp palms against her skirt, she cleared her throat. It was easier to talk to him in the dark. It always had been.

''I need to tell you that I appreciate your staying after all. Truth to tell, I wasn't too excited about being here by myself tonight. I don't believe I've ever stayed in the house alone. Grandmother was always here. And she usually had servants who lived in as well. It's only in recent years that she made do with dailies.''

Rand gazed out over the dark lawn, relaxing in the rocker. In the distance he could see the glimmer of a light. The nearest neighbors weren't close. Margot would have been all alone had he not remained. Yet her admission caught him by surprise.

"Rand?" she said.

"Yes?" Even her voice sounded achingly familiar in the dark. She had loved to talk once they were in bed. She said the cloak of darkness made it easier to share her thoughts and feelings. He remembered he'd shared more with her than anyone else in his life.

In the end, it hadn't been enough.

"I did think about you after I left." She gave a ghost of a laugh. "It's dumb, but I really thought you'd come after me and tell me to come ho—back."

"Sorry I wasn't fast enough," he said tightly, reaching down to gather his bags and briefcase. "I'll take these in. Did you finish reviewing the papers in the study?"

He refused to hash over the past. It was long gone. Would she have returned with him if he had followed her immediately, instead of trying to reach her by phone first? Or was she just trying to put the burden on him. He hadn't flown immediately to her side and so she didn't want to have anything to do with him? If she'd just once taken one of his calls. Or agreed to see him when he had finally followed her to Natchez.

He straightened. He would not dwell on the past. He already felt the stirring of the old anger. At her. At himself for choosing to believe they had a chance at a life together, that he'd ever be able to support her like her grandmother had. He thought he'd moved beyond that anger, but being around her proved him wrong.

"I glanced at them. Nothing at all about my parents. I'll check in her bedroom in the morning and see if there is anything there. After that, we can tackle the attic."

"Good night, then."

"Didn't you want to talk to me? Georgia and Shelby are gone."

He hesitated, then shook his head. "Not tonight. I need to call my secretary and find out what's happened during the last two days at the office."

"Of course, business always comes first. Don't let me keep you."

Business he could deal with. But Rand was beginning to wonder if he could ever deal with Margot. How had a simple errand to get her to sign a few papers turned into a weekend's stay and his promise to help on a futile quest? Why hadn't he talked with her tonight? It wasn't as if they had a future together. The sooner he told her why he'd come, the better for both of them.

Margot sat on the veranda until quite late. The monotonous creak of the rocker soothed her nerves. She and Rand had not said much, but more had been revealed this evening than during all the weeks after the loss of their precious baby. She placed her hand over her stomach as if she could still feel that small presence. She'd miscarried in the fourth month. Just a week or two after she'd first felt the flutter of life. One terrifying afternoon, she'd lost their future. Rand had rushed to her side from work and at first seemed just as devastated as she felt.

But by the time she returned home from the hospital, he was already back at work, staying longer than ever before. Even going into the office on the weekends. When she needed love and comfort the most, he closed himself off from her—finding his own solace in work. Or maybe he'd always found that special something with his job, and turned to it when she'd let him down.

Shivering slightly in the warm night, Margot decided Rand's presence caused the old memories to flood. Memories made bittersweet with the passage of years.

Tomorrow she and Rand would talk. Did he

want them to try again? If not, if Rand were staying from some misguided sense of responsibility, she could quickly absolve him of the need. And if in the search they discovered her father had not left of his own volition, it might reaffirm her faith in men. *Her faith in Rand?*

When Margot entered the kitchen the next morning, her grandmother's longtime cook, Caroline, was back—singing a gospel hymn at the top of her voice as she scrambled eggs. Rand stood near the back door, sipping a cup of coffee as he gazed over the shaggy yard. He hadn't heard her enter over Caroline's singing and Margot took a moment to study him.

The pullover shirt he wore displayed his chest and shoulders to advantage. Broader and more muscular than she remembered, she wondered if he worked out, or if her memory was just faulty. Though how she could have forgotten something like that, she couldn't imagine. His hair fell across his forehead, and she once again experienced that longing to brush it back, to tangle her fingers in its thickness, refamiliarize herself with its texture. This time she'd pull his face down to hers...

Blinking she shook her head, forcing herself to erase such thoughts from her mind. The light khaki pants he'd bought wouldn't stay clean long in the dusty attic. She wondered if he'd considered that. Probably not. He'd just bought what he wanted and never mind how practical for the task ahead.

Her own shorts were old, the sleeveless top long past its prime. Both were perfect for the unseasonably hot weather and rummaging around dusty boxes.

"Good morning, Miss Margot. You sleep all right?" Caroline spotted her and turned her beaming face toward her. "I just about got Mr. Rand's breakfast finished and I can make your eggs however you want. Plenty of bacon and sausage, biscuits, grits and coffee. You want some orange juice?"

Rand turned and looked at Margot, studying her with his dark eyes. Face-to-face Margot realized more than his body had changed. There was no welcome in his expression, no special smile just for her. He might as well be a stranger.

A fascinating man, but a stranger nonetheless. The pang that hit her was unexpected.

"Just toast and coffee, please," Margot said, ignoring the hint of disappointment at his lack of greeting. What had she expected? She wasn't exactly thrilled to be stuck with him, either.

Rand stepped into the kitchen and raised his cup. "Excellent coffee, but you need more than that and toast for heavy investigating. Caroline prepared a feast.''

''I guess, there looks to be enough food for a small army,'' Margot said, feeling flustered.

''Nothing like cooking for the gentlemen. They have a hearty appetite and appreciation for good food,'' Caroline said as she made shooing motions. ''Y'all get into the dining room. I'll bring in everything. You want your eggs poached, Miss Margot?''

''So much for listening to me,'' Margot muttered as she turned to lead the way to the dining room. Rand was right on her heels. He caught the door behind him.

''It won't hurt you to eat a good breakfast. We don't want your energy flagging.''

Margot raised her chin and turned to respond, and almost bumped into him. She hadn't realized he was so close. Rand reached out a hand to steady her, his fingers warm as they closed on her bare arm. Swallowing hard she tried to ignore the sensations that exploded from his touch. But that proved impossible. Clearing her throat she looked up at him.

''Toast would have given me enough energy.''

''For everything?'' he asked slowly, his thumb making random patterns on the soft skin of her inner arm. Margot couldn't think.

Nodding jerkily, she tried to pull free. His grip tightened. Without looking away, he placed his cup on the table and reached for her with his other hand. Margot gazed into his eyes, mesmerized as his dark gaze seemed to glow with hidden fires. Slowly she felt herself drawn closer.

Before she could say a word in protest, he pulled her body against his and encircled her with his arms. Lowering his head, he kissed her. Margot stood rock still for a split second before pressing herself against him and opening her lips for his kiss. Her arms encircled his waist and she hugged him tightly. Stars exploded behind her eyelids, and heat washed through her. His scent filled her senses and she tried to find a rational thought that would help her end the madness.

They hadn't seen each other in years. Yet in all that time, she had never found anyone who came close to fostering the feelings this man could with a single look.

She should remember he didn't want her. Somehow that didn't seem important with his mouth plundering hers, with his hand tracing patterns across her back, with his heart thumping heavily against hers.

"Excuse me," Caroline said coming from the kitchen with her arms laden with plates. "You two can carry on like that later. Now you sit yourself down and eat this breakfast while it's still hot.'' She placed the plates on the table—Rand's at the head, Margot's to his right. Fussing with silverware and napkins, she looked over at them.

Margot pulled away, breathing hard, her lips warm and slightly swollen. Her heart raced. For a second she'd forgotten everything but joy.

Only—it was an illusion.

Blinking she stared at Caroline and met the woman's knowing gaze. Flushed with embarrassment, she pulled out her chair.

''Thank you, Caroline, it looks delicious,'' Margot said, trying to recover a semblance of normalcy. She couldn't believe Rand had kissed her again. And kissed her like he was never going to let her go.

Nor could she believe how she'd responded. How she wanted more and resented Caroline's interruption. She should be grateful for the woman's entrance. Kissing Rand did not play into her plans for the future, or even the present.

She took a bite of poached egg, aware of Rand drawing his own chair and sitting close to her. His leg brushed hers as he settled in.

Her gaze flew to him. He smiled at Caroline as if nothing earth-shattering had happened. Margot tried to eat, but the food had little taste.

Her blood pumped through her veins, her breath catching. Why had he kissed her? Twice! He showed up unexpectedly and—what? Offered to help, to stay for a few days. To kiss her senseless?

Rand poured another cup of coffee, raising his eyebrows in silent question to Margot. She nodded and pushed her cup closer to him.

"Tell me about your work," Rand said as he spread butter on a biscuit and began to eat with obvious enjoyment.

Warily Margot studied him. "Why?"

Shrugging, he replied, "I'm curious. Shelby mentioned the other day that you own your own business. I would have thought the garden club, Junior League and hospital charities would have kept you too busy to work."

She stiffened at his sardonic tone. Tilting her chin slightly, she glared at him. "My grandmother may have belonged to those organizations, but I don't. Of course I work. How do you think I've earned my living?"

"I have no idea. I thought you ran home to resume your former life-style."

"I didn't come home because of that," she said, wondering if that was what he'd truly been thinking all these years. Surely he had known her better than that. How could he have thought—

"Come on, Margot, you know you missed this." He waved his hand around the elegant dining room, with the beautiful old cherry wood furnishings, the ornate crystal chandelier suspended from the tall ceiling, the Sevres china and elegant Revere silver coffee service. "Our apartment was a far cry from luxurious."

She shook her head. "You're crazy, Rand. I left because I was devastated at the loss of the baby. And there was no one to comfort me, to stand by me." Not that her grandmother had. She'd dismissed the miscarriage as a trivial incident, one that allowed Margot to resume her proper life without problems. She'd predicted Rand would not come after her.

"And you received comfort from that old woman?" he asked incredulously.

Slowly she shook her head. "No."

"So why stay away?"

"I told you, I didn't think you cared. Besides, I had Shelby and Georgia."

"You thought I didn't care because I didn't immediately come after you? Give me a break here, Margot. I had commitments."

Pushing aside her place, she took her cup and rose. "*I* was a commitment. You married me, remember? And proceeded to ignore me when I needed you most. All for work."

"Margot. I had other—"

"I don't want to hear it! This conversation is pointless. What happened, happened. It's over. I'm going up to Harriet's bedroom to see if there're any papers there. I called Grandmother's attorney and got the name of a reputable appraiser who will be by later today to appraise the furnishings. If you want to stay to help, fine. Otherwise, maybe you should just head back for New Orleans."

Margot left on shaky legs. Any talk of the past disturbed her. Was she ever to feel resolution, closure to the event? She'd been ecstatically happy with Rand until she'd lost their baby. The weeks that followed had been a nightmare. Longing for comfort, for companionship, his absence had been worse than anything. His being here now made a mockery of her feelings. She needed to gain some distance.

Rand finished the meal Caroline had prepared, though he'd lost his appetite. He would like nothing better than to return to New Orleans today. It made no sense staying any longer. They couldn't even eat a meal together in harmony. Nor have any kind of discussion. Not with Margot's running away at every turn. Had he truly expected anything different from her?

Once finished with breakfast, Rand headed for the attic. He found the stack of labeled boxes and chose two from two dozen years ago. He carried them down and dumped them on the floor in the empty bedroom closest to the attic steps.

Margot followed, eyeing him warily. If she could keep the conversation off the topic of the past, she might be able to relax. Rand glanced up as she walked in.

"This is probably a wild-goose chase, you know," he said as he ripped off the tape of the first box. "Harriet could have been talking nonsense, Margot."

"I know that's a possibility. Still, I need to verify it either way if I can."

"You could be opening a can of worms."

"How do you figure that?" she asked as she peered into the box and reached for a handful of paper.

He sat beside her. Close enough for her to reach out and touch him, if she were so inclined. Could she scoot to the left a little? Or would that make her look like a total idiot?

It was a huge room, with twelve-foot-high ceilings, and two pairs of French doors that were open to the upper balcony. But Margot felt as if her space had been invaded. He was too close. Even with the coolness from the early-morning air drifting in the open French doors, she felt warm, crowded.

"What if you learn something you wish you hadn't?"

"Like what?"

"I don't know. What if your grandmother didn't chase your father away. What if he turns out to have been the no-good drifter she called him? How will you deal with that?"

"That is not new. I expect I'd go on like I have. But what if he didn't leave of his own volition, don't I deserve to know that?" she asked, wondering if she could jump up, take her box and find an empty room to herself. Rand's presence was too disturbing.

Taking a deep breath, she tried to calm her nerves. Instead she caught a whiff of Rand's aftershave. Her heart skipped a beat in memory. Awareness flooded her. Shyly she glanced at him from beneath her lashes. He concentrated on the contents of the box, allowing her all the time in the world to study him.

Which wouldn't be enough, she realized as the minutes drifted by. She could stare at him forever. Taking another breath, she turned her attention to the papers in hand. The jumble took her aback. She would have thought her grandmother would have been meticulous in her storage. It looked as if she just dumped in every paper relating to a particular year. Sighing, she began to scan the top sheet.

Rand stretched over and snagged a wastebasket. "Dump the trash in here. And nothing is worth keeping unless it has some value today."

Scanning each sheet briefly, Margot either tossed it into the wastebasket or placed it in a stack beside her.

But before long, she found her mind wandering. She scanned the documents, but her attention focused on Rand. She could see him from the corner of her eye. And for a moment the years seemed to melt away. It was as if they'd never parted. Wistfully she wished things had been different.

Of course she had wished for years that she'd had her baby. That they could have built a family with love and laughter. Would Rand have stayed if the baby had been born, or would he have become so consumed with making it in the business world he would have neglected his family? If she'd had her baby, would she have felt so neglected while he worked? Had their marriage been doomed from the beginning—or did they still have a chance?

He looked up as if reading her mind. "Well?" he asked.

"Well what?"

"What are you doing?"

"Nothing, just thinking," she said uneasily.

"About?" He looked at her curiously.

"Nothing," she repeated, too afraid to broach the subject. That way lay heartache.

"Thinking about nothing gives you that funny look on your face?"

"I don't have a funny look. Did you find anything?"

"I'm not looking, I'm talking with you. For the first time in five years, I might add."

She tilted her chin and faced him. "And whose fault is that?"

"Yours."

"If you are referring to my returning here, I wonder how long it took for you to realize I wasn't at the apartment? I mean, did you notice right away, or was it several days later when the laundry hadn't been done, or groceries bought? You were never home long enough to notice I was missing otherwise."

"Not so. I knew the first night. The apartment was empty, echoing like a tomb."

"Don't." The memory threatened to overwhelm her. She blinked back sudden tears. Five years and she still ached. How long would it take to get over the loss. To get over it and move on?

"Denying it or ignoring it won't get anything resolved, Margot. You can't hide from what happened. We both made mistakes. It's up to us to correct them if we can. And if we can't, then it's time to cut our losses and move on.''

She studied the carpet pattern, wishing she were elsewhere. After the worry about her grandmother, her illness and death, to have to confront Rand was too much. She longed to stop the words, to have him stay another day or two before bringing up the past.

''You're five years too late,'' she said softly.

He drew a deep breath. ''In more ways than one, I guess.''

Glancing up at him, she frowned. ''What do you mean?''

He hadn't meant to bring up the divorce so abruptly, yet what choice did he have? The timing was perfect. He obviously made her uncomfortable. At first he thought it was because of lingering feelings on her part. No longer. It wasn't like him to put off difficult tasks. And this one should be easy.

''You and I never should have married.'' He knew the words. He'd rehearsed them for years. ''Our worlds were too far apart.''

Margot stared at him, tears shimmering in her eyes. She didn't want it to be true. She had loved him so much!

''When we hit our first bad patch, instead of drawing together to fend against the world, we went our separate ways. Did you think I wasn't upset about losing the baby? I wanted the baby myself, Margot! It was a part of both of us.''

He hesitated a moment, then slowly added, ''I hated losing it for another reason. My father had been diagnosed with cancer. He didn't have long to live. I wanted him to see my son or daughter. Wanted him to have the chance to hold his grandchild once before he died.''

''I didn't know,'' she whispered. The hurt grew with each word he spoke, with each memory he exposed. She hadn't known about his father. That made their loss all the worse.

''No, you didn't know, or you wouldn't have fled. The apartment wasn't as fancy as this place, but if you had stayed around, the money eventually came in.''

''It was never about money!'' She rose up to her knees and dashed away the tears that threatened to spill over. ''It was about needing someone there for me. You were gone, I was alone—so alone. My God, do you have any idea how difficult that was for me? At least here I had my sisters, familiar places. A time to recover. I wasn't alone!''

Rand looked away, frowning. ''I needed work to cope. I was totally helpless. There was nothing I could do to make things right. So if I buried myself in work, it took my mind off—''

''And I needed something, too, Rand. Only I

had *nothing*! Nothing to consume me so I wouldn't remember, wouldn't feel. Just an empty apartment, an empty nursery, an empty spot on your side of the bed. So I came home. You're right, obviously we shouldn't have married. I expected more than you gave me. I needed more.''

His hard gaze clashed with hers. ''And I expected more, as well. Loyalty and commitment.''

''Don't talk to me about commitment. You were so far gone in your work that you didn't have time for anyone!''

''It was the only way I knew to deal with the tragedy.''

''And what about me?'' she almost screamed.

He was silent for so long, Margot thought he wouldn't respond. Her breathing slowed, her flare of anger began to fade. Finally he spoke.

''I let you down in more ways than I thought.''

Deflated at his capitulation, she sank back on her heels, at a loss for what to say next. He admitted he'd let her down? She should have felt vindicated. Instead she only felt a huge sense of loss. She had loved him, believed he loved her. And their marriage had not stood the first test.

''It's over, then, isn't it?'' she said slowly.

"No more hoping you'll show up one day, no more wanting to turn back the clock, make things different."

"Honey, you can't make things different. You had no control over the miscarriage. I didn't know how to comfort you. I couldn't find comfort for myself. Maybe your returning home was the best thing for you."

Standing, Margot dusted her hands and looked at him. "The best thing for me would have been to have my husband come for me five years ago." With that, she left the room.

CHAPTER FOUR

RAND watched her leave, anger simmering just below the surface. She still had the power to infuriate him!

He rose and took two steps toward the door, intent on following her. Then his cell phone rang. Reaching into his pocket, he withdrew the slim device. Flipping it open he growled into it.

"Marstall."

"Whoa, boss. Don't snap my head off. Am I interrupting something important?" His secretary's familiar voice came clearly through.

"No. What's up?" Betty Jean wouldn't call if it weren't important.

"We received a fax from Bendix. You said to let you know when it arrived. Do you have a fax machine there?"

"Send it to the laptop. I'll go plug it into a phone outlet. What does he say?" Rand asked as he began walking toward the bedroom he was using. In seconds Margot's abrupt departure was forgotten as he concentrated on a crucial aspect of his business. Setting up his laptop, he noted his suit jacket slung over a chair back—the divorce papers still in the inside pocket. Why not just give the damn papers to her and have done with it?

It was over an hour before Rand finished dealing with the myriad details related to the Bendix fax. That done, he went grimly in search of Margot. Surprised, he found her in the bedroom where he'd deposited the boxes. By the looks of the overflowing wastebasket and stack of papers beside her knee, he could see she'd been at it for some time.

She glanced at him, immediately returning her attention to the sheet of stationery she held, saying nothing.

Rand sat beside her and reached for another stack of papers. He'd cooled down while working through the Bendix mess. Now, despite all that had transpired between them, he was determined to discover more about Margot before leaving. What had she been doing over the last five years?

"You never told me about your business," he said a few minutes later.

She looked up in surprise. "I opened a small interior design place. I have two women helping me. There's plenty of work." She flicked her gaze into space for a moment as if considering what else to say.

"I bet you're a huge success," he murmured, tossing a stack of papers into the trash and reaching for more.

She cocked her head to one side and looked at him with some surprise. "Why would you think that? I had no business experience. My major in college was fine arts—which I never finished, as you know."

"I thought you might have gone back to school."

"No." She looked back at the papers in her hand, not wanting to give anything away. Especially how listless she'd felt for most of that first year after they'd separated. She'd had no energy, no enthusiasm. Just living through the day had been almost more than she could manage. College had been the farthest thing from her mind.

"I expect you are a success because of the flare you have of making something out of nothing. You made our place a home with very limited materials and no money to speak of," Rand said, frowning as he tossed another small stack of papers into the trash. "I imagine with the kind of money you can charge your clients, you could work miracles."

Margot felt a touch of warmth at his unexpected compliment. "You liked our apartment?"

He looked at her. "Of course I liked it. It was welcoming and warm." Like you, he almost added. He wouldn't tell her how he'd systematically dismantled it, and moved when he finally accepted she was not returning. It had become a mockery of the too brief happiness they'd shared and he couldn't bear to live there without her.

His current place overlooked the Mississippi and cost six times what their small apartment had. It had been decorated by one of New Orleans's trendiest interior design firms—and didn't have a tenth of the warmth Margot had created for them.

Not that he needed that. He wasn't home enough to even care. Business kept him busy.

"That's nice of you to say, Rand. I never knew," Margot said sadly. She wished that she had known he felt that way when they'd been together. She'd tried so hard to make their apartment a home. She'd loved it herself, but had never realized how he felt about it.

"Do you still live there?" she asked softly, a remembered fondness for the place sweeping through her. It had been her first home. Her apartment now had never felt the same. Beaufort Hall would never feel the same.

Rand shook his head. "I live in the Arts District. Have a place that overlooks the river."

"Much more suitable to your life-style, I'm sure," she said stiffly. Another indication of his success and of how far he'd gone in his quest to move up. For a moment she wondered what his place looked like. Sleek and modern, she'd bet. With black and gray and chrome. Sighing softly, she looked at the bottom of the box. They were through the entire year's papers and found no mention of her father or mother.

"Nothing," she said, looking at the dust that covered her shorts, rubbing the grime on her hands.

"Nothing in that year, let's try the earlier one. When exactly did your father leave?"

"I don't know. I was so little. Obviously sometime before Georgia was born, but I couldn't tell you exactly when."

They opened the next box, from twenty-four years ago, and began to delve into it.

"Where do you live now, Margot?" Rand asked. He had an address; the detective he'd hired provided that. But he wanted to hear from her what it looked like, where it was located.

"Near the center of town. I have a place on Sixth Street."

"A showcase for your business?" he guessed.

"No, actually, I decorated it before I started

the business. Early secondhand. It's nothing special.''

He raised an eyebrow. That was unexpected. ''Why?''

''Hmm?''

''Why secondhand?''

''I didn't have much money when I was starting out and needed every penny for the business. It's home now, so why change things just to change them?'' she asked. ''I don't have to please anyone but me, and it suits me.''

''Your grandmother must have had a fit.''

Margot laughed softly and nodded, looking up to share her amusement. ''Actually, she did. You know how crucial appearances were to her.''

He remembered. He hadn't fit Harriet's ideal. But he was older now, and a bit wiser. ''Did she come from a poor background? Maybe that's why money and class distinction became so important to her.''

''Is that why you find it important?'' she asked.

He raised his eyes until he stared into hers. ''I wanted more than what I started with. Doesn't everyone want to better himself?''

''Maybe, but that's no reason to ignore your family or fight against what's important to them.''

"Are we talking about Harriet or me?"

She shrugged.

"I never married you for money or position."

"Why *did* you marry me?" she asked, holding her breath for the answer.

Because I loved you more than life itself, he thought suddenly. He'd thought she hung the stars. Only to find at the first sign of trouble, she scooted back home and turned her back on him, on that love. On their future.

"It seemed the thing to do at the time," he replied, holding her gaze with his own. Wondering again why she'd married him. As an escape from her grandmother's domination, he'd often thought.

"What about love?" she asked so softly he almost missed the words.

"Love's an illusion, a transitory emotion best left to teenagers and dead poets."

For a long moment she couldn't speak. Her throat ached. She felt the sting of tears behind her lids. The sadness of the years weighed her down. They'd had so much when they'd started out, how could it ever have gone so wrong?

She licked her lips and looked away. "I should have figured it out then, huh? Especially when you were gone all the time," she said at last.

"Why do you think I worked such long hours? Went without so we could save money to get ahead? I wanted the best for you and instead was only able to give you a third-floor walk-up apartment that contributed to the death of our baby."

"No! I told you last night that had nothing to do with it."

Margot wanted to say something more about the past, but couldn't find the words. The loss was too great. The longing was something she constantly lived with. She couldn't talk about it.

"Miss Margot?" Caroline appeared in the doorway.

"Yes?"

"The appraiser is here."

"I'll be right there." Scrambling up, she wiped her dusty hands on her shorts, knowing she must look a mess. Well, she wasn't out to impress anyone. She glanced at Rand and then looked away. His gaze was fixed on her legs and for a moment awareness swept through her. Thankful for the interruption, she hurried downstairs.

Rand watched her go and reluctantly returned to sorting. He had to focus on his reason for being here and not get sidetracked. Margot had become even more beautiful over the years, maturing into a lovely woman. The hint of sadness and mystery in her eyes, her graceful walk, the elegant way she moved her hands when talking only captivated him more. And he didn't wish to be captivated.

It proved difficult to concentrate on the task at hand when he had a million questions he wanted to fire off. The primary one being why had she turned her back on him, on them? Why hadn't she given them a second chance? Or were the old suspicions true? Had she seen him as an escape from Harriet only to decide the change wasn't worth the price?

Restless with the pointless questions, he rose and went back to the attic. They'd be finished with that second box in no time. He brought down two more. He thought it extremely unlikely Margot would find anything incriminating in her grandmother's papers, but he was willing to go along with her for a day or two. By Sunday, he had to get her signature and head back for New Orleans. His company would only run itself for so long.

Margot returned a few minutes later, frowning. "He said it may take weeks to get everything appraised. And when I mentioned the attic, he upped it by another week."

"Is there any rush?"

She shrugged. "Not really. I thought a couple

of weeks would see everything wrapped up.
Then I could get back to my normal life.''

"Living in your apartment, running your
business.''

She looked at him sharply. ''Yes. I'll be glad
to get back to my own place.''

"What did you and your sisters decide about
the furnishings? Are you going to sell everything with the house?''

"No. Georgia and Shelby told me which
pieces they want. The rest I'd like to offer clients. I can leave them here temporarily. Some
pieces are quite valuable. I may be able to use
them in restorations or decorating. I expect the
house will take some time to sell. There's not
much market for a huge old antebellum house
with all the upkeep it demands. When it sells,
any furniture left unsold can be put in storage
until I find buyers.''

She sat gingerly near the open box, keeping
her distance from Rand. ''There are some very
beautiful antiques. I can offer the buyer a history of each piece. Harriet told us about them
often enough.''

A soft chirping sounded.

"What's that?'' Margot looked around, puzzled.

"My phone.'' Rand reached into his back

pocket and brought out his thin cell phone. Flipping it open he spoke into it. "Marstall."

Betty Jean's voice responded. "I know you said nothing short of an emergency, but we've got a problem with the grain shipment from the West Coast. There's some holdup and Joe isn't sure if we can afford the delay. The container ship is scheduled for a run to Osaka after this and the timing is getting tight."

"Have Samuels handle it and update me when I get in."

"And that will be?"

"Monday."

"For sure, boss? I've rearranged all your appointments and meetings for this week. Don't stay longer, it'll play havoc with your calendar."

"That's why I pay you the big bucks, to keep things running smoothly."

She laughed. "Right. I'll remind you of the big bucks scenario come raise time. What are you doing there, boss?"

"Right now, sorting through papers from twenty years ago," he said dryly. "I'll see you Monday."

"Do you want interim updates on this situation?"

"Monday."

He flipped the phone closed and slipped it into his back pocket.

"I guess we should be glad that's the first time they needed you, huh?" Margot said dryly.

"I've been in touch since I've been here."

"I'm not surprised. Couldn't let something like a visit interrupt your work, now could we?"

"I run a big company, Margot," he said evenly.

"And it's the most important thing in your life, right?"

"It is now."

She dragged one of the unopened boxes and turned her back to him. He almost smiled at the childish gesture. But her words echoed in the silence.

His work *was* important. It was the only steadfast certainty. He apparently was not good at relationships—witness his own marriage. But he was outstanding in business endeavors. His rise in the shipping industry had been nothing short of meteoric.

Margot ripped off the old tape and opened the box. This one was from the year her mother died. Quickly she scanned the pages, sorting, discarding, consciously ignoring the man behind her. She heard the pages ruffle as he worked, and fought the temptation to shift her position so she could see him. Gradually her anger abated. She'd known he was a workaholic from the early days. Why rail against fate? Rand was as he was. At one time she'd supported his dedication, his long hours to build a career. She'd been so proud of him.

But it all changed when she lost the baby. She needed him more than ever, and he stayed away from home all the time. What had been tolerable before had turned incomprehensible, unacceptable.

And yet, she still wondered about him. How did he spend his days? And nights?

No!

She refused to acknowledge interest in someone who put work above a grieving wife.

So focused was she on denying any interest in Rand she almost missed the letter. Only after it was in the discard pile did the words register. She snatched it back. Reading it carefully, she felt the first stirring of enthusiasm.

"Rand, listen to this," she said excitedly, her momentary pique forgotten.

"It's a letter from—" she turned it over to find a signature "—someone named Edith. Sounds like she was a friend of Harriet's, listen. 'My dear Harriet. I still am so distressed at Amanda's passing,'" Margot looked up briefly. "Amanda was my mother."

Rand nodded. "I remember."

Margot continued, "'But I suspect you know that. When I think of those three motherless children, I want to weep. And especially because it need not have happened. No matter what you say, I firmly believe your meddling in that marriage was a contributing factor to Amanda's giving up. You were a fool to attempt to play God. She loved Sam and he adored her. The fact he had no money, or family to suit you, was always immaterial. I wonder if your conscience lets you sleep at night.'"

Quickly Margot skimmed ahead. "The rest of the letter is about some mutual friends. Then she ends it as 'your longtime friend, Edith.'"

Her eyes shining, Margot looked up. "That's the proof. Harriet did do something!"

"It could indicate that."

"But what? Did she drive him away, or did she just meddle in the marriage until he got fed up and left?" she asked, studying the letter again as if it could provide the answer.

"See if there are any more letters from Edith."

"Grandmother probably severed all ties with the woman after that letter. I'm sure she didn't like being taken to task for her behavior. Odd she kept it, isn't it?"

"Unless the other information in the letter

was of importance to her. But I'd say it was odd. Yet she probably never expected you to go through these boxes and discover it.''

Margot nodded in agreement. "I would never have bothered if she hadn't said that before she died. I want to see if I can find anything else.''

"You can't make this too important, Margot. You may never discover the truth," Rand said.

She looked out the open French doors, gazing over the garden, the stately oaks green and lush, gray Spanish moss dripping from some of the limbs.

"Learning the possibility my father didn't abandon us shook my world," she began slowly. "I thought one of the truths of my life was that he had. I thought everything my grandmother ever told me was the gospel truth. To find out that was such a monumental lie makes me wonder if other things were lies. And if so, what? But the most important part is that maybe my father didn't leave of his own volition, that he didn't deliberately abandon me. I almost can't imagine how that would affect my view of the world. Of relationships.'' She darted a quick glance at him.

"And if you find out he didn't want to leave, what then? He's had years to contact you after your mother died. And never did. Gone is gone.''

She shrugged. "He could have been killed, moved across the world. Who knows why he didn't get in touch. Maybe there was something Harriet held over him to prevent his trying. It almost doesn't matter. Just knowing he didn't leave but was driven away would be enough. For me."

"And will that be enough for Georgia and Shelby?"

"What do you mean?"

"Aren't you curious about the man? Don't you want to know where he is, if he's still alive? What he's been doing these last twenty-three years?"

She thought about it seriously for a long moment, then slowly shook her head. "That's not as important. Sure, if he walked in today I'd be interested in meeting him, talking to him, finding out what he has been doing all this time. But the important thing to me is the *knowing*."

"You need more than papers your grandmother may have saved," Rand said. He rose and raised his hands high over his head, stretching out his back. It had been years since he spent hours sitting on a floor. A run would help, but it was too late in the day. In this kind of heat, dawn was the time to run in Mississippi. It was too hot now, and would grow even hotter before the sun set. Maybe this evening.

"What else should I be doing?"

"Talking to contemporaries of your mother or your grandmother. See if anyone else has a clue to what happened. For all you know the situation was common knowledge twenty years ago."

"My grandmother never spoke of it. And changed the subject if we ever brought it up. Besides, if it were common knowledge, wouldn't someone have told me by now?" she asked, trying to keep her gaze on his face, but she couldn't help be intrigued by the muscles in his arms and chest as he stretched. He looked solid and big and formidable. Not the striving young man she'd married. He'd come into his own.

For a moment she felt the sharp prick of regret that they were no longer together. Did he ever have regrets that he had turned his back on her and let her go?

Did he see other women?

"Now what?" he asked, looking at her sharply.

"Huh?"

"You have the most peculiar look on your face. What are you thinking about?"

"Nothing." She looked down at the letter again.

Rand stepped across the boxes, dodged the

stack of papers now spilling over from the trash and hunkered down beside her. He reached out a finger and tilted her face up to his. "What?" he asked softly, commandingly.

"I was wondering if you dated other women," she threw out, amazed at her temerity. It was none of her business.

She was his wife, but they hadn't shared a life since—

"No, I don't date. I'm married, remember? Though I guess I'm still surprised that's so."

"What do you mean?" She tried to ignore the spiraling sensation of awareness his touch started. She wished he'd move his hand, yet craved his touch the way a thirsty man in the desert craved water. Gazing into his eyes, she saw the lines around the edges that hadn't been there five years ago, and a poignant realization hit her. They were growing older. Life was moving ahead and the once bright dreams they shared no longer had meaning.

"I would have thought Harriet would have prevailed upon you to divorce me years ago."

"She tried."

"And?"

Knocking his hand away, Margot stood and took a couple of steps toward the balcony. Rand followed. She wanted to turn and run. He was so close she could imagine the edge of her shorts brushed against his chinos. His breath stirred the air around her face. Swallowing hard, she faced him and gave a halfhearted shrug. "I didn't want a divorce. It was my independent stand against her. She couldn't force me."

"And now?" His voice hardened a bit.

"Miss Margot, you and that man coming to lunch? I don't want to throw it out," Caroline called up the stairs.

"We'll be right there," Margot yelled back, grateful for the interruption. She didn't want to talk about divorce, or marriage or anything. She started to leave but Rand caught her arm. "We still need to talk, Margot."

"Maybe, but I have a million things to do now. And Caroline is the only one left to help out around here. I don't want to alienate her or I'll have to do everything."

"Being a few minutes late to lunch won't alienate her," he said dryly.

She pulled her arm from his grasp and started walking. "Maybe not, but we can talk later."

Margot did her best to avoid Rand that afternoon. She called into her office. When Rand made a comment in passing about die-hard business owners, she flushed. She was as involved in her business as he was in his. But she could put it aside for family, she thought defensively.

If she needed to. Wasn't her presence in Beaufort Hall proof?

By dinner, Margot had convinced herself she could spend time with Rand and discuss whatever he wanted rationally without becoming emotionally upset. But did she want to? If given the opportunity, would she consider changing her life? Maybe she and Rand could still build some kind of marriage. Not the way she first expected, but a different kind of relationship. She had her work now. He had his. If her expectations were lower, if she didn't ever plan to risk another pregnancy, could they build a future together?

Was that what he wanted to discuss? He was staying to help her find the truth about her father. Didn't that show some interest on his part?

By dinner she was ready for the discussion, whatever it entailed.

They would eat on the veranda, in the shade of an old oak tree. She didn't want to eat formally in the dining room every night as her grandmother had. Showering and changing into a pink-and-white sundress, Margot was pleased to see some color in her cheeks. She was still too thin, but maybe the dress would camouflage that fact.

Rand had also changed his clothes, she noted

when she joined him on the veranda. He looked wonderful.

"Did you get a drink?"

He raised a glass half full of amber liquid. "Iced tea suits me. Can I get you something?"

"No, I'll wait for dinner and have tea as well." Feeling almost shy, she crossed the veranda to the table Caroline had set. It looked lovely, set with crystal, fine china and silverware. She touched one plate lightly.

"When we were children, Harriet would never use this china. It's Limoges, you know. She said clumsy little girls had no appreciation for the finer things in life. So we ate off different china."

She lifted the plate and held it up, looking at Rand with an imp of mischief. "I could smash it now and there would be nothing she could do about it."

He nodded. "You could, but why bother? She wouldn't know about it, either."

"I guess." Slowly she put the plate down. "We didn't have such a great childhood," she said slowly.

"So I'm coming to find out."

"I used to love to hear you talk about your childhood."

"It wasn't so great, either. We were dirt poor

and hard-pressed sometimes to have food on the table.''

"But playing in the river, exploring the bayous with your friends, the way your family celebrated the holidays, it sounded like a Brady Bunch family to me. I often wondered what my mother was like. Had she been raised the same way, or had Harriet felt she'd done things wrong with her and changed her tactics with us.''

Margot looked at him uncertainly. ''She wanted each of us to marry into families with pedigrees back to the Mayflower, and with money to burn.''

"And instead, you married me.''

She nodded, her gaze dropping to the place setting. The silence seemed endless.

Raising her eyes, she found Rand's gaze steady on her. She should say something else, but her throat closed and she felt tears welling. Why had they let happiness slip through their fingers? The years since she'd last seen him seemed so lonely, so empty. Nothing had changed, but the sadness that filled her was almost more than she could bear.

"I fixed fried chicken and all the trimmings,'' Caroline said, wheeling a tea cart loaded with bowls and platters out onto the veranda. "Now both of you eat up. Don't want this food to go to waste."

"Cold fried chicken is good the next day," Rand said, holding Margot's chair. She sat and blinked to dispel the tears. She refused to let them spill over.

"We got plenty other things to eat, don't have to be eating leftovers," Caroline grumbled as she began to serve dinner.

It was growing dark by the time they finished. Rand sat back and sighed, a grin lighting his features. "Best eating I've had in a while."

"Do you cook for yourself?" Margot asked, curious about how he lived. Curious about a lot of things.

"No, I eat out mostly, or nuke a TV dinner."

"I once thought that would be fun, to eat out all the time. But when I first started my business, I did that a lot, and it got old fast. I'd rather have a cup of chicken soup in my own apartment than endless meals out alone. I like my own company."

Rand nodded. The time was right. He knew enough about negotiating to know he'd probably never get a better opening. She was not pining for things she couldn't have, nor making overt attempts to reinstate herself in his life.

"Want to walk along the levee?" she asked.

"It's not too dark yet, and it's pretty along the river in the evening."

"Fine." He rose and followed her as she wound through the overgrown gardens and up a short pathway to the top of the levee. The Mississippi River drifted lazily by, the water dark and muddy. Most of the light had faded from the sky, stars were showing in the eastern horizon. Before long it would be pitch-black.

"And when the last of twilight fades, what will keep us from plunging into the water?" Rand asked as they headed up the levee.

She laughed softly. "There's going to be a full moon soon. It should peek out over that way in only a little while. With the clear sky, it'll give us plenty of light. We don't need city lights for everything," she mocked softly.

"Honey, you're talking with a country boy. Never even saw the city until I was fourteen."

She smiled. "I remember. Stick with me, I'll make sure you don't fall into the river," Margot said, reaching out to take his hand.

It was a mistake. She knew it as soon as her fingers grasped his, as soon as she felt his fingers slide between hers and his hand grip hers firmly.

The sensations that danced along her nerves had nothing to do with keeping them safe, keeping from plunging into the river. They had to do with love and desire and longing. With memories of things that should have been locked away and only let out in the darkest of midnight in the privacy of her room.

Instead, once again past and present seemed to mingle and Margot had trouble differentiating between them. She had loved him so much, and had grieved his loss as much as their baby. More—she had never seen her baby, never held the child. But her arms ached for longing when she slept alone. And hope had died slowly when he never came—or attempted to contact her.

But there was anger mixed up in her feelings, anger he hadn't cared enough to come after her. Anger that he'd so easily let her go. If he'd walked out on her—

But of course he had. He'd turned his back and focused on work to the exclusion of everything else. She had not gone after him. Should she have stayed? Should she have returned after the worst of her grief had eased and forced a confrontation between them? Fought harder for her marriage?

For the first time she looked at her *own* behavior. For years she'd considered herself wronged. But had she also wronged Rand? Marriage was a two-way street. She had waited for him to come after her, but the conviction suddenly hit her—maybe *she* should have gone after *him*.

"Margot," he began.

"Rand," she mimicked, turning to look at him. Were they being offered a second chance? Was there time to see if they could make a go of it? She'd put away foolish, girlish romantic thoughts. She could enter into an alliance with more realistic expectations now.

"You asked me if I ever thought about you. I thought of you often after you left," he began.

"I thought about you all the time," she confessed.

"I'm afraid to ask how you thought about me."

Should she tell him the truth? Would it matter now after all the years?

"I was angry at first," she began.

"I could tell," he murmured dryly.

"Hush, I'm telling this and don't need interruptions."

He smiled in the darkness. She always liked to talk in the dark. Maybe it had something to do with the way her grandmother raised her. She had to be so proper and controlled where people could see her. But under cover of darkness Margot could let her true self surface. Had he made a mistake not coming for her after dark, he wondered whimsically.

"I needed you and you weren't there," she said.

"When?"

"All the time," she said. "When I lost the baby, I wasn't even home from the hospital an hour before you left. You were at work when I woke up and when I went to bed at night. At least, I thought you were at work."

His hand tightened on hers. "Where else would I have been?"

"I don't know. It just occurred to me maybe you were not just working, maybe you had—"

"Had what?"

"Other needs? Others who could help you through that time?"

"If you are asking about other women, say so."

"Okay, was there someone else?"

CHAPTER FIVE

"MARGOT, you are the most exasperating woman I've ever known. I can't believe you'd ever think such a thing!"

"It's not hard. Why else would you be gone all the time?"

Rand dragged his fingers through his hair and turned to stare at the slow-moving river.

"I blamed myself for the loss of our baby. If I had had more money we wouldn't have lived there. Throwing myself into work was my way of dealing with the situation. Next time, I vowed, there would be no third-floor apartment. You'd have the best care money could buy!"

"I told you living there had no impact. The doctor was clear there was nothing we could have done. That precious baby was just not meant to be born. I railed against fate for months, inconsolable! But that didn't change anything." She stopped for a moment, then took a deep breath. "I loved our apartment. It was my first real home."

"And that wasn't," he said nodding back toward the mansion.

"No. It was a place I lived with my grandmother. It was her home, her avocation almost, but just a place for me to stay while I was growing up. Our apartment was the first place I truly felt at home."

He ducked his head trying to see into her eyes. "I never knew that."

She shrugged. "You should have. I did all I could to make it nice for us."

"It was a home, Margot. And cold as ice once you left. I couldn't stay when I finally realized you weren't coming back. Everything there reminded me of you."

Margot knew she owed Rand the truth she'd just realized.

"I shouldn't have waited for you to come after me. It was my marriage, too. I realize now that I should have fought for it. But at the time, I thought that if you came after me it would prove that you cared."

He sighed and rubbed his eyes with his thumb and forefinger. "I don't think I could offer you enough assurances. I tried, but obviously failed."

Slowly she reached up and touched his cheek lightly with her fingertips. "I was young then, Rand, only twenty-one. A kid really. And kids that young shouldn't have to face life-and-death problems like we did. I was too young to know that time gradually heals everything—even the loss of a baby. Though not completely. I wake sometimes in the night, did you know, and think I hear an infant crying. My arms longed to hold that baby, my heart still aches with the loss. She would have been almost five, starting kindergarten in the fall.''

"So you think it was a girl?"

"I don't know. Sometimes I imagine a little boy."

"Don't think about it, Margot. It'll tear you apart if you keep dwelling on it."

"I know that. I discovered that in the first months afterward. But sometimes I just can't help myself."

He drew her into his embrace, holding her close to his heart, rubbing her back slowly. It was meant to comfort, Margot knew. But the feel of Rand's arms around her didn't soothe, but excited. She drew in a breath, surrounded by his scent, enticing and male.

She wanted more than comfort. She wanted affirmation that he had thought about her over the years. That he had wanted her with the same longing and remembered fever with which she ached for him.

She tilted up her head, wishing that it wasn't

so dark, wishing she could see his expression, look into his eyes and see what he was feeling.

"I'm glad you came after all," she whispered.

When he lowered his face to kiss her, she responded eagerly. So familiar, so different. She kissed him with all the longing of five long empty years. Giving no thought to the future, Margot plunged herself into the present. She'd been too long without the feel of a man's arms around her, without the exquisite zinging in her blood, without the sensations that brought her to life as nothing else ever had. She had missed Rand, and his touch, his special excitement.

The kiss went on so long Margot lost track of time and place. Rand anchored her to earth, or carried her to the stars, she wasn't sure which. Eons passed, or time stood still. They were alone in the world, or in a world of their own making where everything was possible, and nothing had the power to hurt.

When Rand slowly lifted his head, searching her face, touching her lips lightly, she was dropped back into reality.

"Come to my room, Margot," he said, his hands molding her to him.

Shocked at the suggestion, she hesitated. There was so much between them. Nothing had changed. Would taking such a step he proposed solve anything? Or make it worse? Yet when he held her, she could scarcely think. Only feel. Feel the pleasure he always gave her. Feel the fire in her blood that ignited only when he touched her. Feel connected, safe, free.

How could anything be worse than the separation they'd endured? Maybe it was time to let go of the past and try again. Excitement flared. Swallowing hard, feeling daring and alive for the first time in years, she slowly nodded.

They walked back to the house, awareness between them strong, the knowledge of what they were about to do acting as an aphrodisiac. Despite the darkness, Margot found the path with no difficulty, feeling as if she were floating above the sandy surface.

Not two minutes earlier she'd wished for more light, but the brightness in the house seemed harsh after the soft starlight on the levee. For a moment she panicked. Did she know what she was doing? She hadn't seen Rand in five years. They had separated under the worst of circumstances.

But when he brushed his lips against hers again, she knew the fever in her blood couldn't be quenched. She had so little, a night in his arms would hurt no one. Even if he didn't stay, even if business proved a stronger pull, she'd have one more memory. A happier one, to replace some of the sad ones.

He led her into his room and shut the door. With a muffled oath, he snatched her close and hugged her so tightly she could scarcely breath. This was where she belonged. Did Rand also know they belonged together? He couldn't be so loving if he didn't feel it, too.

When he picked her up and gently laid her on the bed, Margot forgot to think. Ignoring her doubts, she knew only that she wanted him more than anything. Craved his touch, longed for the passion she knew she'd find in his arms. The past was gone. Maybe they could forge a new future together.

As he came down on the bed beside her, she smiled shyly and reached out to draw him closer. For the first time in years, Margot felt she'd come home.

The chirping of Rand's phone woke her. It was just after dawn, and the sky was a soft blue. Cool air stirred through the open French doors. Margot rolled her head and looked at him, her heart kicking into overdrive. He lay beside her in the bed and looked so dear she could scarcely breathe. She wanted to find the phone and smash it to smithereens. He'd wake up any second and be drawn into the call from his business.

He opened his eyes and gazed into hers.

The chirping sounded louder, more insistent.

"Good morning," he said, brushing a kiss across her lips.

Before she could respond, Rand rolled over and sat up in bed, reaching for the phone. The move dislodged the sheet and Margot scrambled to pull it over her. This was not how she'd envisioned waking up!

They'd made love more than once last night, yet the bold light of day made her feel as shy as their first time so long ago.

"Marstall," he said. "And this had better be good or you're fired."

Betty Jean had been with him for almost five years. She knew when to call and when not to, but frustration was building. One glance at Margot and he knew she had the same thoughts she always did about his work. And this time he wasn't sure he could blame her.

"Boss, it's not good. One of our oil tankers has run aground near Baltimore. The captain says it's pilot error, but the local harbor pilot, of course, says it was our fault. You need to get back here. Joe can't handle all the details and Martin doesn't have your clout. He's preparing a statement now."

"Damn!" He pushed back the covers and stood, walking to the window. It was just after dawn, far earlier than he had wanted to wake up.

"When did it happen?"

"Just a few hours ago. Early morning in Maryland. I got a call when they couldn't locate you."

"Which ship?"

"The *Betsy Ross*."

"Any seepage?"

"None noted."

"Thank God for that. I'll be there as soon as I can make it."

"Sorry to cut your weekend short."

Rand didn't even reply; he just disconnected and turned to look at Margot. The frown on her face assured him she had heard his comment and was clearly unhappy.

"I have to go," he said.

"Go," she said, looking away. Her hands fisted against the sheet.

"Margot be reasonable, I didn't plan this! One of our tankers has run aground. I've got to get to the office to monitor the reports and begin damage control. Once we assess the damage, real and potential, we can make sure we do all we can to minimize any environmental impact."

"So go," she said. "There's no one here stopping you."

"Look at me, dammit." He strode over to the bed and leaned across it, putting his face almost against hers. Slowly she turned and looked at him, her eyes wide and impassive.

"Don't pout," he said, wanting to kiss those slightly swollen lips, change her frown to that slumberous look she got when they made love. He wanted her again, but there was no time.

"I'll be back as soon as I can," he said, leaning another few inches and brushing her lips with his.

"Don't bother," she said. "I can finish my search on my own. And I certainly can manage my own life without your help. I have for five years."

Rand straightened and ran a hand through his hair in frustration. He didn't have time for this. He had a different, more immediate crisis to deal with.

Turning, he reached in the drawers for a change of clothes. He still had a couple of new shirts and another pair of chinos. He headed for the bathroom, his mind already spinning with the information he needed, preliminary plans for damage control.

Margot waited until he closed the bathroom door before venturing from the bed. She found her sundress in a puddle on the floor where she'd discarded it last night. Drawing it on, she looked at the tousled bed. Last night had been wonderful. If his office hadn't called, would they have made love again?

Nothing had been said about the future, but before falling asleep, Margot had envisioned today differently. Instead of reading musty old papers, she would have suggested a long picnic in the lazy afternoon sunshine. Maybe dinner and dancing in Natchez, she thought wistfully.

''Daydreams aren't worth the paper they're written on,'' she quoted wryly.

Turning resolutely, she knew she couldn't daydream away her life. He was leaving. That was no surprise.

She knocked against the chair holding his suit jacket. As it slid to the floor, she smiled sadly. When they'd lived together, he'd always slung his jacket on the back of any available chair, leaving it to her to hang it in the closet.

Sighing wryly, she admitted old habits were hard to break. She reached down to pick it up. A batch of folded papers fell from his inside pocket. Her name on the partially folded sheet caught her eye. Slowly she picked up the pages and opened the packet. Skimming the front page, she sank to the edge of the bed in shock.

Divorce papers!

Stunned, Margot carefully read the top sheet. It was a Petition for Divorce. Rand had started steps to divorce her!

Embarrassed heat flooded her as she realized what a fool she'd been. She'd been entertaining thoughts that they might try to get back together, might try to make their marriage work. Instead Rand had come to ask her for a divorce!

An incredible hurt began to sweep through her. He'd used her. He had never hinted at the real reason for his visit. And, gullible as a teenager, she'd gone along with his every suggestion.

Gone along? She'd practically thrown herself at him. No wonder he'd said nothing.

"I'll call you—" Rand stopped in the doorway, his eyes on her face. When he dropped his gaze to the papers in her lap, his expression closed.

"You'll call me about the divorce? Was that what you were going to say?" she asked. Slowly her hand rose to massage her heart. She knew it was breaking—again.

Was that possible?

"Margot, honey, I—"

She rose, enraged. "Don't honey me, you lying rat! You never did say why you showed up this week, did you? What was last night about? You came here for a divorce. Was last night just a final fling?'' She threw the papers at him. Rand didn't move and the sheets drifted to the floor. Margot stepped over them as she stormed for the door.

"Don't leave!" he ordered.

She turned to glare at him. "I don't have to leave. If I wait long enough you'll do that for us, right? Go to your precious business. And don't ever come back."

"Margot."

"Shut up!" Horrified at what she'd discovered, horrified she could have misjudged the situation so much, Margot spun around and ran down the hall to her own room, slamming the door shut behind her as the tears spilled over. She had not cried in front of him. A small victory, but all she seemed to have right now.

Last night had been glorious. But only for her. He'd come for a divorce! Feeling betrayed, she crossed the room to her own bathroom, locking the door behind her. She had no reason to think he'd come after her, his track record proved that. But just in case. She reached for a towel and sank on the edge of the tub. Her heart was breaking. Sobbing, she tried for control. It was too much. Too much.

"Margot." He rapped on the door, tried the knob. "Margot, let me in."

She held her breath, trying to stop the tears.

It wasn't like Rand to come after her. Didn't he have to be at work? Wouldn't his precious business fold without his constant attention?

He knocked harder on the door. "Margot, I can't leave you like this."

She took a shaky breath, fighting for control. "Go, Rand. Go away."

"Margot, this is a major crisis. I have to be there."

"Go away and don't ever come back."

Endless minutes passed. Tears welled again, spilled over her cheeks. She blotted them with the damp towel. She couldn't go through this again. Why hadn't he told her that first afternoon? Why let her begin to dream about—

"I have to go, but I'm coming back. You can count on that."

The day dragged by. Margot ignored the stack of papers awaiting her. Ignored the other tasks that had to be done to prepare the house for sale. By dinner, she'd accomplished nothing. Sinking listlessly on one of the wicker rockers on the veranda, she waited for Caroline to call her to supper. The late-afternoon air was still and hot. Idly staring at the overgrown yard, Margot ignored it all. Her emotions were all topsy-turvy—anger, hurt, regret. How could she have allowed herself to be tempted by Rand?

How could she help it? He tempted her beyond restraint, obviously. And for a little while she forgot the past and gloried in the present. It had been too long. Shaking her head, she vowed to forget him. He had returned to his first love, one with whom she could not compete. The sooner she got things squared away and returned to her own life, the better she'd be.

And that included forgetting how irresponsibly she'd behaved last night.

The phone rang. Despite her newfound intentions, her heart leaped. Was it Rand?

She went swiftly to the hall phone. "Hello."

"Hi, sis, how are you doing?"

Trying to ignore the flare of disappointment, Margot forced some enthusiasm into her voice. "Georgia! I'm doing all right. The appraisers came yesterday. They started on the living room. There's a whole battery of them, since each of them has a different area of expertise. I thought they could do it in a few days but they say it may take weeks."

"Rand still there?"

Margot went still. "No," she said shortly.

"Oh. I thought he was staying through the weekend, at least."

"There was an emergency at work. And work always comes first with Rand."

"So, uh, did you and he talk some."

"Of course," Margot said dryly, knowing where her sister was heading. "He was a guest in the house. Did you think I'd ignore him?"

"I mean about, you know, your marriage. About getting back together."

"Nothing's changed." Except for her entire world being turned upside down in the space of one night. But Margot didn't plan to tell anyone that. Especially not romantic Georgia. She'd be crushed to learn Rand had arrived solely for a divorce.

"I have a couple of days off in the middle of next week. I can come up and help you sort things, or whatever," Georgia said.

Margot was tempted, but suspected she should refuse. She didn't want to tell her sisters about their grandmother's revelation until she knew for certain whether it were true or not. Until then, it would be better for her to do the sorting.

"Not much to do," she said. "I'll be going back to the shop on Monday. Then I'll go through things here in the evenings. We can't do much until everything has been appraised and valued for probate. Once that's done, I'll have the items you tagged shipped if you like."

"No, I'll come up with a friend who has a truck and bring them down myself. There's not that much. You sell the rest of that stuff and make us a mint! Shelby and I'll do our share spending all that lovely loot. No sense cluttering up my small apartment with grandmother's antiques. I don't like the memories most of them would bring.''

Georgia chatted for a few more minutes before hanging up. Margot was almost smiling, her sister's call had raised her spirits.

Glancing up the stairs, she was tempted to go to Rand's room. She wondered for the hundredth time what Rand had done with the papers she'd thrown at him that morning. She ought to go up to see if they still lay on the floor or if he'd taken them back with him.

The phone rang again making her jump.

''Hello?''

''Margot?'' It was Rand.

Immediately she tightened up, the urge to slam down the receiver strong. How perverse, she wanted him to call, but now she was afraid of what he would say.

''What?''

''I wanted to see if you are all right.''

''I'm fine. Goodbye.''

''Wait! I thought you'd like to know about the situation here. The ship is stuck high and dry but we dodged a bullet with no oil seepage. We're off-loading the oil now to another tanker.

Once done, the next high tide should float the ship free and we can assess it for any damage.''

"I'm glad the oil didn't spill.''

"Yeah, me, too. The thing is, I have appointments this week that I really can't postpone.''

"So?''

"So, I can't be with you for a few days.'' The edge to his voice warned her he was losing patience.

"I don't expect you to be with me at all, Rand. Your conscience is clear.'' She hated the cold finality in her tone, but she'd been badly burned once by this man. She'd be living in a fool's paradise to ever allow herself the slightest glimmer of hope that things could be different.

"I will be back as soon as I can make it.'' The sincerity almost convinced her. Almost.

"You have no reason to come back, Rand. Goodbye.''

Slowly, despite his protest, she lowered the receiver. Waiting ten seconds, she lifted it and lay it beside the base. No more calls tonight. By tomorrow he'd be so caught up in his work he'd forget all about her.

Giving into curiosity, Margot climbed the stairs and went to the guest room Rand had been using. The door was open, the bed made. Obviously Caroline had not let things slide. The room looked immaculate. There were no papers anywhere.

So, she wondered as she headed back downstairs, had he taken them to use for an excuse to see her again? He could just mail them. Or maybe she'd see an attorney this week and start her own proceedings.

The following weekend Shelby arrived to help with the task of closing Harriet's home. Margot had thrown herself into her own work during the week to forget about Rand. She was glad for her sister's company, strongly tempted to tell her about her suspicions, about the wild tale Harriet had told. But she refrained as she had with Georgia. No sense all of them worrying about what Harriet might or might not have done just yet.

They packed up their grandmother's clothes and donated everything still serviceable to a women's shelter. Going through her books they'd put aside the first editions and other valuable pieces to sell. The rest, and Margot was surprised at how many books there were on the history of Mississippi and Louisiana, they donated to the library.

Shelby refrained from bringing up Rand's name until supper on Sunday.

"Heard from Rand?" she asked, sitting opposite Margot at the dining-room table.

Margot shook her head, and deliberately took a bite of the delicious shrimp salad Caroline had prepared.

"Georgia said he'd been called back unexpectedly because of some crisis?" Shelby persisted.

Margot nodded, taking a sip of iced tea. She reached for a hot roll and began to butter it.

"Margot," Shelby said exasperated, "what's the scoop?"

"No scoop. He came, helped out until work called, then left. End of story."

Shelby thought a moment, watching her sister carefully. Shaking her head slowly she said, "There's more. Spill it."

Margot considered it. She truly thought she could tell her without breaking down, without revealing how for a few brief hours she'd thought about changing her life. But she didn't want her sisters to feel sorry for her. Not a second time.

"That's it. Did I tell you that the attorney called me on Friday? I asked him to get all the papers together that I need to sign. There's something else he wants to discuss with me, something that just came up apparently. I'm to see him on Wednesday."

"You told me that yesterday. If you don't mind handling it, Georgia and I will be guided by whatever you decide."

"I don't mind. I can't think of what he wants to talk about. I wish the appraisers would finish so we can list the house. Do you think it will sell fast?"

"Nope, for all the reasons you mentioned earlier." Shelby glanced around the elegant dining room and wrinkled her nose. "One of us should have felt some attachment to this place."

"Do you ever wonder what our lives would have been like if our father had not left?" Margot asked slowly.

"Deserted us, you mean? When I was little I used to pretend he came back and took us away from Harriet. And let me stay up late to watch TV."

Margot smiled. Maybe she wasn't the only one affected by their father's absence.

"I always felt it was my fault he left," she said.

Shelby laughed. "That's dumb, sis. You were about three, right? I was still a baby. How could we have done anything to make a grown man leave?"

"I know that as an adult, but as a kid that's what I thought. And I worried about my bad blood."

"What bad blood?" Shelby asked, puzzled.

"Once I had biology and understood how babies came to be made, and listening to Harriet harp on lineage and bad blood and the mistake our mother made marrying our father, I worried that I took after him and had bad blood."

"Right, like we could believe anything Grandmother said. She was fanatical on the mistake Mom made marrying the man. But she was the only one who thought that marriage was a mistake and only because she wanted her daughter to marry some blue-blooded rich man. And it's evident that our father wasn't rich or blue-blooded."

"I used to wonder if Mama died of a broken heart."

The knocker on the front door rapped.

Shelby looked up. "Expecting company?"

Margot shook her head.

Caroline used the main hall to get to the door. Margot looked at Shelby and strained to hear who it was.

Two seconds later Rand walked into the dining room.

Caroline came right behind him, her face beaming. "Now you just sit down and I'll bring you a plate right away. I know you must be starving with that long drive from New Orleans. We've got plenty of food. And I know you'll want iced tea. Sit right here.'' She pulled out the chair next to Margot. ''I'll be right back.'' With a bright grin, she scurried into the kitchen.

Rand nodded at Shelby, then Margot.

''Good evening, ladies,'' he said, sitting in the chair Caroline had drawn out.

''What are you doing here?'' Margot asked, stunned to see him, stunned at the delight that invaded her senses. She flicked a glance at Shelby who stared in surprise. Taking a deep breath, she pinned a polite smile on her face. ''I didn't expect you.'' She hoped the heat that swept through her didn't show in her cheeks.

Rand nodded, amusement evident in his eyes. ''I told you I'd be back as soon as I could re-arrange it. Finished up everything pressing this morning which frees me up for the next couple of days. Nice to see you again, Shelby. Will you be joining us in searching?''

''Searching?''

''No, Shelby's leaving after supper,'' Margot said, narrowing her eyes in an attempt to head Rand away from that dangerous topic. ''We've done lots this weekend—sorted Harriet's clothes, giving the usable items to a shelter and throwing away the rest. Although we did keep two old dresses to use as rags. We threw out the ones that no one could wear. Dumped her cosmetics and personal items.''

"And the books, don't forget the books, Margot," Shelby said, laughing softly. When her sister looked at her, she raised her eyebrows in feigned innocence. "I don't know why Rand needs a play-by-play account of our weekend, but if you are going to give it to him, be precise."

"Oh." Margot felt like an idiot. Grateful for Caroline's interruption when she arrived with a heaping plate for Rand, she took a sip of iced tea hoping to gain some control over her wayward emotions. Seeing Rand was not conducive to her serenity.

As she studied him, her heart rate sped up. Her mind filled with images of the two of them the last night he had stayed. Today, his dark hair looked windblown. His suit fit perfectly, giving him a distinguished appearance that had her flustered. She had trouble thinking straight. Why couldn't the man have stayed in New Orleans?

She couldn't very well kick him out while Shelby was sitting there. The questions would be endless. But as soon as her sister left, she'd have it out with Rand Marstall. If he'd brought his blasted divorce papers, she'd sign them and send him on his way tonight!

Shelby seemed reluctant to leave. When they'd finished dinner, she suggested they sit on

the veranda for a while. She and Rand easily
discussed the oil tanker that had precipitated the
crisis, then moved on to other topics. Margot
threw in a comment from time to time to keep
her sister from suspecting anything was wrong,
but as the evening progressed she wanted to
scream her frustration. The later it got, the
harder it would be to get rid of Rand. Even now,
it was almost too late for Shelby to reach New
Orleans at a reasonable hour.

"Oh, look at the time, I must go," Shelby
said, as if reading her sister's mind. "This has
been great, Rand. I'm so glad we got to visit
for a while."

Rand stood as Shelby did. "Can I help you
with your bags?"

Acting like he was the host, Margot thought.
If he thought he could start waltzing in and out
of her life at his convenience, she'd soon set
him straight—once Shelby left.

"Thanks, but I only had a small case and put
it in the car before supper. I'd say don't be a
stranger, but I don't think I need to say that
now, right?" she asked, glancing between the
two of them.

Fortunately, Margot thought, Rand kept silent. She gave a small smile and remained quiet
herself. Time enough to explain things to her

sisters later, after she clarified everything for Rand!

"Goodbye, Margot, let me know what happens with the attorney." Shelby gave her a hug and then surprised Margot by giving Rand a brief hug. "See you."

Margot remained silent as her sister started her car and drove down the driveway.

Finally she stood and faced the man who was driving her crazy. "You have a nerve coming back."

"I'm happy to see you again, too, sweetheart," he said, then pulled her close and kissed her.

Margot resisted—for about two seconds. But the seductive pull of his touch proved stronger than her resolve. When his lips moved persuasively, she succumbed and responded. No matter what else happened between the two of them, this never changed. She loved his touch, thrilled to his kisses. Delighted in the feel of the man, in his scent, in the strong beat of his heart beneath her palm, the feel of his hard muscles beneath her fingertips. Shocked with her easy capitulation, she sought the strength to push against that hard chest.

When he released her, she stared up at him, her eyes wide and furious. She wanted to be angry with him, but some of that anger was directed toward herself.

"Don't do that!"

"I like doing that. And by your response, you like it, too."

"That has nothing to do with anything," she snapped, turning to put some distance between them.

"I beg to differ. I think it shows there is still something between us."

"After the other night, I think that would be obvious. But it's only sex." She didn't want to discuss the other night, but better she bring it up first. Maybe she could control the trend of the conversation. "That was never a problem area in our marriage. Speaking of which, did you bring the divorce papers back with you?"

"Not this trip. I want to talk with you, Margot."

"You sound like a broken record. That's all you say. Where were you five years ago when I wanted to talk? There's nothing to say now."

"I think there is. Your response to my touch has me thinking things might not be over. That we might salvage something."

"Like what? You have your work, and now I have a business of my own."

"So maybe you'd understand better the demands of a company. I won't apologize for working hard. I wanted more for you and that was the only way I knew how to get it.''

She spun around at that. ''Oh, Rand, that was never what I wanted. I had grown up with money. It bought *things,* but things are meaningless when a person craves something else. I wanted a family. I wanted to be important to you, have you find me important.''

''I did.''

Remembering her thoughts of a different kind of marriage, she wondered if Rand might be thinking along similar lines A marriage that would allow them to be together, but without the high and unrealistic expectations they'd once had.

''Why, after all this time, do you want a divorce?'' she asked.

He rubbed the back of his neck and loosened his tie. Staring out over the shaggy green lawn he spoke softly. ''I was advised to get one by my attorney.''

She blinked in surprise. ''Your attorney? Why?''

He drew a breath. Waiting impatiently, Margot watched him. The reason couldn't be any worse than the actual demand, she tried to tell herself as her apprehension grew.

''My company is ready to expand. We'll be moving into an entire new strata with the potential to reap a tremendous profit. Alex suggested I take steps to make sure I keep what I earn.''

She stared at him for a moment, until the meaning sank in. ''So rather than take the chance your wife would come storming in to demand half of all that lovely profit, your attorney advised you to get rid of her, now, while you are still relatively poor?''

Rand looked at her, his expression unreadable. He nodded, once, wondering why he'd given into Greg's suggestion. In all the years they'd been separated, Margot had never once asked for a dime. Not that he'd expected her to come to him. She'd had her grandmother's wealth to fall back on. She hadn't needed anything he could give her. The thought rankled.

Even now, once the estate was settled, Margot would inherit one third. The furnishings in the dining room alone would bring a huge sum. He couldn't imagine her ever wanting anything from him. But that didn't mean it wasn't prudent to protect his assets.

''You should have brought the papers...I would have signed them in a heartbeat,'' she said, walking past him and into the house.

CHAPTER SIX

RAND let out his breath in a long sigh. After spending that night with Margot, all the old feelings began to tumble around inside. Could they consider working out some deal where they'd stay married, be together from time to time?

He shook his head. He'd missed her this last week more than he'd expected. Especially at night when he lay alone in that king-size bed he'd bought a few years ago. Instead of instantly falling asleep each night, he'd lain awake and thought about Margot. How soft her skin had felt, her hair like silk. Remembering not just their most recent night together, but others as well.

Closing his eyes, standing on the veranda surrounded with the scent of sweet olive, and despite the cool breeze from the river, he swore he could still smell Margot's fragrance.

Spinning around, he went to his car and withdrew the large suitcase. Time his wife learned who she was up against. He was staying until they'd hashed everything out and came to a resolution. He hoped it would be one he'd want to live with.

Margot heard Rand's steps on the stairs, the sound of a door closing. He was staying. For a moment gladness filled her, then anger that he wouldn't listen to her. She was puzzled as to why he planned to stay despite her obvious lack of welcome.

He could be ruthless, determined, focused on whatever goal he set for himself. Look how he'd risen from his poor beginnings to the successful man he was today. So successful his attorney feared for his wife's greedy hand in his affairs.

Dressing quickly for bed, Margot slipped between the sheets and snapped off her light. Lying alone in the dark, she felt the siren pull of Rand's presence only a few doors down the hall. Closing her eyes for sleep didn't help. Behind her lids, she saw that night just over a week ago. She imagined she could still feel Rand's fingertips against her skin, his lips on hers. She kicked off the sheet, suddenly hot. But the gentle air stirring from the open French doors caressed her skin as his kisses had.

Rolling on her side, she curled up into a tight ball, wishing her mind would go blank.

"Margot?"

The soft voice came from the upper balcony that surrounded the house.

"Go away, I'm asleep," she muttered, trying to ignore the pull of attraction.

"Come out and talk to me. There are advantages to this weather. The night is lovely, balmy and quiet, and I'm too keyed up after that drive to sleep."

"That's not my problem," she said, but sat up. Where had she put her robe?

"Come talk to me in the dark," he coaxed.

"In the dark?" She found the robe, slipped into it. Flicking her hair out of the neckline, she tied it tightly. The floor felt cool beneath her feet as she stepped out onto the wooden balcony. Rand leaned against the railing, dimly lighted by the stars and the moon that had risen a short time before.

"Why bother to talk. I tell you to go and you ignore me," she said.

"Or, I tell you I'm staying and all you do is argue."

She shrugged and crossed to the railing, careful to keep a wide distance between them. "We didn't used to argue."

"You used to chastise me for being away for long stretches."

"I told you I wanted a husband, not a large paycheck."

"I remember taking long walks together along the Mississippi," he said softly, moving closer.

Margot nodded, eyeing him warily. She remembered them, too. Hands entwined, shoulders brushing as they strolled along the riverwalk and spoke of dreams and plans. Such happy times. The familiar ache began.

"If I tallied all the things I liked about being married to you, it would probably take me until Thursday," he said whimsically.

Margot looked at him in astonishment. That didn't sound like her ruthless businessman. "What an incredibly nice thing to say!"

"It's true. And I could tally what I didn't like in two sentences. I regret not having enough money to give you a life similar to the one in which you'd been raised. And I regret each minute I spent away from you."

Staring in disbelief, Margot could scarcely trust her ears. Was she hearing him correctly? The honeyed words caressed her, soothed the ache.

"Then why didn't you come after me when I left?" she asked. If he had truly cared, how could he have let her go?

"You mean immediately? I was hurting, too.

Did you think I didn't love that baby we'd made? Did you think it meant nothing to me to lose it? To know I wouldn't be a father after all. That I wouldn't be helping my child to grow and learn. To see the wonder in his or her eyes as all the magic of living unfolded?''

She shook her head.

"I wanted to do something, but when I tried to talk to you, you'd just shake your head and change the subject. You shut me out, Margot."

"I didn't shut you out," she protested, even when the doubts arose.

"It sure seemed like it."

Margot felt dazed. She thought he'd *wanted* to stay away. Was his obsession with work truly the result of a wife who had turned from him? She'd been so devastated, so inconsolable. Losing her baby had been the hardest, most tragic event of her life. And she'd felt so alone. How could she not have known her husband was grieving as well; that he needed more from her than she offered?

"I'm so sorry, Rand."

He nodded. "Grief does different things to different people."

"We should have known that. Maybe—"

"I spent a lot of my free time with my folks after you left. And with my mother after my dad died. She is a wise woman. She helped me work through the grief of losing you and the baby. Too bad the young aren't taught that before we need it. It would make life a lot easier.''

Margot wrapped one arm around the tall pillar and gazed toward the river.

''You were lucky to have your mother. Harriet kept telling me to get over it and move on. My sisters were no help, except to be there for support. It was so hard. Even today—''

''I know, the echoes of a crying baby when you awake in the dark.'' He stood. When his arm encircled her shoulders, Margot let go the pillar and rested against his chest. It felt so good to be held. To be able to tell him some of what she felt.

''Even today the desolation creeps into me.'' She realized something else. ''I understand now how work can provide a kind of numbing solace.'' Hadn't she used her own business to try to forget Rand this week?

''With all your mother talked to you about, did she ever suggest you see me again?'' Margot asked, curious despite herself.

He shifted on the railing, turning to lean against it, drawing her into the circle of his arms, into the V of his legs.

''Not after that last rejection. She said maybe I was beating a dead horse and it was time to let you go.''

"What last rejection?" she asked. "I never rejected you."

"What would you call refusing to take my calls, not answering my letters and having a maid tell me you were not home when I'd seen you enter the house only moments before?" he asked evenly. "I call that blatant rejection."

Margot felt confused. She leaned back in his arms searching his face. "Rand, I don't know what you're talking about."

Instantly Rand realized. "Dammit! Harriet!" he said angrily.

"What?"

"I called here that first evening when I got home and found you gone. Harriet answered the phone and told me you didn't want to talk to me. I called every day for two weeks. I told you I had commitments. I couldn't leave, but I sure as hell called! Either Harriet or some maid named Naomi answered the phone. The message was always the same—you didn't wish to speak to me. I left endless messages asking you to call me."

Margot shook her head, horrified by what she was hearing. "No. Rand, that's not possible. No one gave me any messages." She clutched his arms. This couldn't be true.

Grimly he nodded. "Margot, I called you daily for over a month, came by three times and sent you at least five letters—and you know how much I hate to write letters.''

Swallowing hard, she knew her world had just been shaken again. And by her grandmother's machinations. ''So you did come after me?'' she said, trying to take it all in.

''Three times. I wanted to see you, to talk to you, hold you. Hell, I was dying inside. We had lost our baby and then it looked as if I was losing my wife. Each time that Naomi answered the door she said you weren't at home and she didn't know when to expect you.''

''You should have challenged her story.''

''I did the time I saw you enter just ahead of me. I pushed my way inside. Harriet showed up. Your grandmother said you blamed me for everything. Your infatuation had worn off and you wanted out of the relationship! When I heard nothing from you as the days went by, I began to believe her.''

Margot sagged against him, resting her head against his chest. Futile anger surged. How had she dared? Harriet knew how much she missed Rand. She'd argued with her about it for weeks.

Tears welled. Her heart had taken another blow. How could her own grandmother have conspired to keep her from her husband?

''I started to return home a few weeks after coming here but she convinced me it would be a mistake. If you cared anything about me, she insisted, you would have contacted me. In a strange way, it made sense, so I went along with it. For a long time I didn't think too clearly. I was so grief stricken.''

Rand placed a finger beneath her chin and raised her head, resting his forehead on hers.

"We were both deceived.''

"And our lives changed because of her.'' Guilt began to build. She should have contacted Rand, fought harder for her marriage. After five years was it too late? "I can't believe it. How dare she play God like that!'' Margot said. The jumble of feelings that tumbled around exhausted her. She didn't know what to believe. But she knew with certainty that Rand wasn't lying to her now.

"So where do we go from here?'' she asked, feeling bereft of everything, uncertain, unsure, numb. Nothing in her life was proving true. Had her feelings for Rand been true? Would she discover that she could love him again? Or would the fear of loss, fear of his turning away, of putting work first always stand between them?

"Where do you want to go from here?'' Rand asked, releasing her and resting his palms against the railing.

"I'm not sure. I need some time to think about this. I feel as if my life has been turned topsy-turvy.'' And his letting go chilled her. If he cared wouldn't he say something?

"But there's more, right?" he asked.

Margot hated to respond. She wished she could slip back into her bed and pull the covers over her head. Try to discover how she really felt about all this. But she owed Rand honesty, at least. Especially after her grandmother's lies.

"Rand, you came here a couple of weeks ago to seek a divorce. I'm willing to sign the papers to grant you that divorce," she said slowly. "I certainly wouldn't contest it."

"Why?"

She had startled him, she could tell.

"It's all a jumble, but I think it would be the right thing to do. The best thing."

"For who, you or me?"

"For both of us. We had a wonderful seven months. I loved being married to you, loved every moment until I lost the baby. But that's gone. Things have happened to change us. We aren't the same people we were five years ago. And my grandmother did a horrible thing."

"You are not responsible for her actions. Or did your love die with the baby?"

"No. Not then."

"But later?"

"I don't know," she said, distressed anew. Had her love died because she thought him uncaring? Or had it only lay dormant—awaiting his touch, his presence to spring to life again. Why couldn't she think straight?

He was silent for a long time.

"Very well then, Margot. But if we are getting that divorce, I think we should make some memories to last us down the long lonely years." He swept her into his arms and kissed her. When he raised his head, she was breathless.

"Sleep with me tonight," he urged.

She was tempted. Standing in the circle of his arms, she felt she could forget everything— the past, the present and the future. But she couldn't spend the rest of her life in his embrace. And she had to get her own life straight before she could think of any future.

"Rand," Margot began. She mustn't do this, not again. She could *not* make love with him tonight and say farewell in the morning.

"Hush," he said as his mouth came down on hers and swept away the doubts.

"I can't, Rand." Pulling free, she fled to her bedroom and shut the French doors with a bang.

Margot awoke early. For a moment she was disoriented, until memories rose. Rand had tried to seduce her so sweetly. If she'd agreed, would they have made love far into the night? It seemed so real she could almost feel it. Should she have agreed? Who would it hurt?

Only herself.

She pushed back the sheet and rose, no more comfortable with her thoughts than she had been when she'd finally fallen asleep last night.

Rand leaned against the wall near the top of the stairs, waiting. Margot spotted him the instant she left her room.

"Sleep well?" he asked.

"Fine." She refused to confess how long she had stayed awake reliving his kiss, wishing she'd had the courage to agree to his suggestion for making memories.

"I heard Caroline a little while ago," she said as they descended the stairs. Nervous, she looked at him from the corner of her eye. He seemed totally in control, not a bit disturbed by her refusal to sleep with him again. Swallowing hard, Margot hoped desperately that her own demeanor looked serene and unconcerned, not flustered and regretful.

Once seated with breakfast before them, Margot smiled brightly. "Tell me about your company."

He looked at her knowingly, then complied and told her how he'd leveraged his assets until he'd attained controlling interest in the shipping firm.

"I can't believe you got the financing. It sounds so scary. What if you hadn't succeeded?" she said at one point. It sounded complicated, daring and extraordinarily perilous.

"Nothing worth achieving is done without risk. There was a lot involved, but I relished the opportunity. It kept me from thinking about the baby, or you. It was my chance to move ahead. Without it, I'd still be a long way from my goal."

"If it had failed..." she began, thinking how she worried over her own business.

"If it failed, I knew I could get a job somewhere. I would have been in debt for the rest of my life, but that was a price I was willing to pay to grab the chance."

And that was a basic difference between them, Margot thought. She needed more security. More than Rand could give?

Build a memory, he'd said last night. Were bittersweet memories better than none? She wasn't sure. She only knew as she sat beside him this morning, felt his magnetic attraction, that she had second thoughts about her refusal.

Her heart skipped a beat. Dare she risk her emotions again? Could she take a chance and refuse to sign the divorce papers, see if they could build some kind of life together? Would he even consider such a suggestion?

"So what's on your agenda for today?" she asked. "How long are you planning to stay?"

He frowned for a moment. "Aren't we going to review more papers? Sort through your grandmother's files?"

"I need to go to work today. As soon as I finish eating, I'll dash upstairs and change and head for the shop. I have commitments, too, you know."

"Role reversal?"

"What?"

"Didn't you claim I was always leaving you when you wanted me at home? Today I thought you'd be here and we would continue sorting Harriet's papers, instead, you're leaving."

"This afternoon, maybe. But this morning I have to go to work."

"I can understand that."

"Was that a snide comment that I should have been able to understand it as well when we were together?"

He raised an eyebrow and shrugged. "Not really. But maybe you should think about it."

"Too busy," she said, pushing back her chair. Walking swiftly to the stairs, Margot breathed a sigh of relief. She wasn't up to bantering with Rand first thing in the morning.

Once dressed, Margot descended the wide stairs. Rand stood on the veranda with his coffee. Looking at Margot when she exited the house, he let his gaze run over her from head to toe.

"You look stunning," he said sincerely.

Her trim red suit fit her like it had been designed for her, the color went well with her skin and dark hair. Her slim body appeared sleek and feminine—and sexy as hell.

He felt a surge of desire. He'd like to take her back upstairs, close the curtains and slowly strip off that sexy suit and see how well the white of the sheets went with her skin. He'd make slow love to her all day, watching as her eyes darkened, as color blossomed in her cheeks. As her scent filled his senses.

For the memories.

Who was he trying to kid? Her? Himself? He still had feelings for her, pure and simple.

"How long will you be gone?" he asked, careful to give nothing away.

"I'll be home for lunch. I'm sure you can find something to do until then. Unless you need to return to New Orleans?" She stepped off the veranda, heading for the garage and her car.

He watched her go, noting her unease. Her lips were rosy and still slightly swollen from his kisses last night. She wouldn't meet his eyes. Smiling smugly, he called after her.

"I'll check in, but I've already delegated most of the routine tasks. I'll bring down more of the boxes and see where we stand. Did you and Shelby make any headway?'

"I told you, we just did Harriet's clothes and some personal items. The appraisers finished in that room, so we were able to accomplish a lot." She kept walking.

"Did you tell her about your suspicions?"

"No."

Rand watched her approach the corner. Once around it, she'd be out of sight. "And when do you plan to do so?" Did she feel as foolish as he did, yelling back and forth?

"When I know something for certain." With a quick glance in his direction, she turned the corner and was lost from sight. A couple of minutes later, he watched her car head down the driveway with a sense of satisfaction. He'd seen her smile and wave.

When she returned home shortly before one, Margot was surprised to see two unfamiliar cars in the driveway in addition to Rand's.

Entering the house, she heard the murmur of voices. She ran lightly up the stairs and headed for the source—coming from the bedroom where the boxes were. Entering, she paused in the doorway and stared at the sight. Rand sat in one corner, a large trash can beside him, stacks of papers were in disorderly piles everywhere. In another corner an unknown young woman also sorted. Straight ahead in the center sat a middle-aged woman, meticulously skimming papers.

"What's going on?" Margot asked.

Three pairs of eyes looked up.

Rand rose from the floor. "Ladies, this is Margot Beaufort. Margot, meet Wendy and Stella. They're helping us sort."

Margot looked at the huge trash cans brimming with discarded papers. Empty boxes were piled haphazardly along one wall. They'd obviously made a lot of progress.

"Could I speak to you, Rand?" she said calmly, stepping back into the hall.

He followed a couple of seconds later.

"What are they doing here and who are they?" she said in a low voice. What had he done? Broadcast her grandmother's actions to the world?

"I hired some help. These women came from a temporary agency. We should be through everything by the end of tomorrow."

"I didn't want half the town knowing about this," she hissed.

"Relax, Margot. One of the guarantees of the agency is discretion. And neither of these women had even heard of your grandmother. They're not reading any more than necessary to save personal papers and discard the rest. Don't worry, Harriet's memory will still be sacrosanct.''

"I don't care about her memory. It's my family's business I don't want broadcast to all of Natchez.''

"It won't be.''

"You should have asked me,'' she said, mollified a little by his assurances.

"You weren't here. It's efficient.''

"And costly, I bet. How much?''

"Nothing for you to worry about.''

"You're not paying.''

"Why not, I called them. I can afford it. You're worrying about nothing, Margot. Accept the help and let's get on with it.''

"I suppose we're to feed them,'' she said, not wanting to examine how disappointed she was to not have Rand alone at lunch.

Stepping back, as if to distance herself from her own thoughts, she frowned. For the entire morning at the office she'd succeeded in relegating Rand to the back of her mind. It wasn't fair now that they had the afternoon together she had to share him with two strangers.

"Caroline can feed them on the veranda and

you and I can eat inside, if you like,'' he said easily.

"No, that's dumb. It makes more work for Caroline. I'll go change and be ready in five minutes.''

The work did go faster, Margot had to admit later that afternoon. Wendy and Stella were efficient and hardworking. By five o'clock, most of the boxes had been emptied. Only a few remained in the attic at the end of the day.

"We'll finish those ourselves tomorrow,'' Rand said after the women departed. ''Then the time-consuming part starts. You have to read all the correspondence they separated. You know what you're looking for. But at least you'll have everything in chronological order.''

"What if there's nothing?'' she asked, looking without enthusiasm at the stacks of paper.

"You tell me, Margot. Can you live with the conviction that she interfered in your parents' lives as she did in ours and somehow caused your father to leave without ever finding the proof?''

"I don't know. It's hard to believe, even after learning what she did between us.''

"She was a difficult woman, convinced her way was right. And ruthless in attempting to make sure everyone conformed to her ideas,'' he said harshly.

"I know." She closed her eyes, feeling memories of the past press down on her. "She was a difficult woman to live with. I never met her expectations. Neither did Shelby or Georgia. But I don't think it weighed on them as much."

"Because you sheltered them from the full brunt of her personality?" he guessed.

She shivered. "Maybe. I was the oldest. I had to take care of them when Mama died."

"And because you felt guilty your father had left."

She shrugged. That guilt had been relegated to the past. The guilt that plagued Margot now was her own part in the demise of her marriage. She should have returned to Rand. She should never have listened to her grandmother. Why hadn't she trusted herself and the love she once felt for this special man?

Caroline served dinner on the veranda.

Rand seated Margot, then sat across from her.

"Do you always eat outside when it's warm?" he asked as they ate the delicious Shrimp Creole the cook had prepared.

"No. Actually I've only eaten out here since Harriet's death. She insisted on using the dining room once we were old enough to not spill at every meal."

"Ah, and you prefer a less formal setting?"

She nodded, thinking about their apartment. She'd avoided any hint of pretension, or elegance. It had been colorful, warm and relaxing. None of the furnishings had matched, but they all went well together. And it had been designed for comfort, not for show.

Her apartment in town reflected a more mature blending of styles and fabrics, but essentially captured a similar feeling of warmth and comfort rather than the more austere elegance of Beaufort Hall.

"How long are you staying?" Margot finally asked after finishing her meal. Now that he had her consent for the divorce, there was no reason to remain, was there?

Except to make some more memories. She felt her face grow warm and quickly reached for her glass of iced tea in hopes of hiding the fact.

"In a hurry to see me leave?"

"No, but with all the demands you have, I expect this isn't easy—being out of touch in Natchez when so many things are happening in New Orleans."

"I can take a day here or there," he said dryly.

For the first time in a long while, Margot felt content. When Caroline brought out Bananas Foster and coffee for dessert, Margot decided to take each minute as it came. They discussed everything from movies they'd both seen recently, to books read. Margot was surprised Rand went to the movies, but she hid it. She didn't know when he found time to indulge, but apparently he wasn't totally consumed with work.

Who had he gone with? she wondered at one point. Then the conversation had veered to his parents. Margot expressed her regret at learning of his father's passing shortly after she last saw him. She could hear the sadness still in his tone. Rand had succeeded far beyond anything his father had achieved, but he'd loved and respected his father and it still showed in his voice.

"And your mother is living in Florida now, you said."

"She has a nice house there. Took some of the furniture she and Dad had, and then we bought new things for her. We could have used your help in setting her up. But it's nice," he said.

"She's happy there?"

"Loves it. Has a bridge club and a touring group. Even does Jazzercise. At least she let me do something for her. Dad never wanted much beyond what they had. And while he was living, Mom didn't, either. But she did allow me to buy her that house and furnish it. I wanted to do more."

Margot longed to reach out to touch him.
Bitterly angry at her grandmother for robbing
her of that freedom, she clenched her hand into
a tight fist.

"They had a happy home. I remember thinking that each time we visited," she said softly.

"But not a lot of material things. They didn't
even have a microwave," he said.

Margot laughed. "Your mother loved to
cook. The convenience of a microwave would
have been lost on her. Things and money aren't
necessary to make people happy."

"Easy to say when you've had it all your
life."

Margot started to tell him she'd been totally
self-sufficient from the time of their separation
until the present, but didn't. It was an old ar-
gument, and not one she could change by
words.

"Do you miss your old home?" she asked.

"Not particularly. I like New Orleans.
Why?"

"I wondered if you did, you seem so surprised we want to sell Beaufort Hall that I
thought maybe you might have wished to keep
your family's home."

"I could have bought it, Margot, when my
dad died. But Mom didn't want to stay there. I
certainly never planned to move back. So she

sold it and now has a nice nest egg for the future.''

''That's what Shelby, Georgia and I will have upon the sale of Beaufort Hall. A nice nest egg for the future.'' She swallowed hard and fell silent. She didn't want to think about the future tonight. Not while Rand was still here.

''I can give you a nest egg as a settlement,'' he said slowly.

She stared at him with horrified eyes. ''No! I don't want anything. Rand, you made all that money, risked everything to buy into the company. And did it all after we separated. I'm not entitled to any of it.''

''Sure you are. It was acquired while we were married.''

''I don't want anything!'' she repeated.

''I'd feel better if you took it.'' He'd done it for her, after all.

''If you keep up talk like that I'll refuse to sign the papers,'' she threatened.

CHAPTER SEVEN

THE night sounds were a quiet background to the lazy murmur of the river. Margot took a sip of the dark chicory coffee, wishing she had not brought up the divorce. She wanted to savor the peaceful evening, one of her favorite times of the day. And savor the darkness. It was the best time to talk, share confidences, draw closer.

She remembered sneaking into her sisters' rooms, sometimes all three of them gathering in one room, against their grandmother's strict rules. The spice of the forbidden only adding to their delight. They'd share dreams and plans for the future, always in the darkness. Georgia would curl up against her when she was very young. Shelby always wanted to be on the edge of the bed. Margot liked being in the middle, as if being surrounded by those she loved would buffer her from the fears and uncertainties that plagued her.

"Tomorrow I'd like to see your shop," Rand said.

Margot started in surprise. "Okay. Want to come in with me in the morning?"

"No, I'll come along later. I need to check in with my own office before heading your way. Shall we plan on lunch in Natchez?"

"Sure."

Was he making plans now because he didn't intend to try to persuade her to share his bed tonight? she wondered? Not that she should expect it. Last night could have been a wonderful memory to treasure down through the years. Only something deep within her argued she didn't want just memories, she wanted the real thing.

"It's still early," Margot said. "I guess I have time to start reading through those old letters and papers."

"Want help?"

"No." She did, but thought it prudent to spend some time apart. She didn't want him to think she couldn't manage things on her own. She'd grown up a lot in the years since they'd been together. She could manage.

It was only a couple of hours later when her eyes began to blur that she wished she'd said yes. His presence in the living room as she read would have kept her company. Now she felt alone. A common feeling over the last few years, but not one she liked.

Rising, she straightened the two piles, read and unread—the unread still much larger than the other. But Margot had discovered more about her grandmother. And every speck of information led her to believe more strongly that Harriet Beaufort had been a ruthless manipulative woman—determined to get her own way in everything she wanted.

But there were no clues about her father.

She switched off the light and wandered out into the grand foyer. The front door was locked. The rest of the ground floor in darkness. Only the chandelier over the stairs remained on.

Slowly, quietly, she climbed the stairs. Caroline had departed immediately after supper. Rand must have closed up and retired for the night.

She entered her room and quickly dressed for bed. Opening the wide French doors to the balcony, she looked at the empty expanse. Had she expected him to be there? To sweep her off her feet and carry her away to a world of private delight? As she slipped into bed and pulled the light sheet over her, Margot admitted she had.

Late the next morning, Margot impatiently glanced at the wall clock again—for at least the fifty-third time. Last night Rand said he would come by the shop this morning. It was after eleven. She had expected him earlier, even though they had not settled on a time. Once again she surveyed her small domain. The cream and burgundy decor pleased her eye, giving the room warmth yet conveying a feeling of spaciousness, which the small shop definitely did not have. On the long side wall she'd hung enlarged photos of successful commissions. She was proud of the work she'd done, and it paid to advertise—even in her own shop.

In the second room, fabric samples, carpet samples, other items necessary for her business were neatly stacked awaiting the next consultation.

Would he be impressed with what she'd accomplished on her own? Or find it small and unimpressive?

Not that she needed Rand's approval, she thought defiantly. She was proud of what she'd done, and that was enough.

Where was he? If Jessie hadn't been there, Margot probably would have started pacing by now.

Rand parked near the address Margot had given him. Slowly walking along the street, he noted the upscale boutiques and trendy shops that lined the avenue. He saw Margot's place and hesitated. Curious about what she'd been doing, he surprised himself with the ambivalent feelings he experienced. Once he had wanted to take care of her, give her everything. But that had been before she left. Her departure had been a major blow and her refusal to speak to him had nailed shut any hope of a reconciliation.

She had never made the attempt to return to him. And even now, seemed agreeable to signing the divorce papers. Had he misread the entire situation? She'd set up her own business, and could provide for herself. She didn't even want a settlement from him when she signed the papers. Not that she'd need anything after Harriet Beaufort's estate was settled.

Now he was going to see her where she spent her day. Margot had never cared enough to come to his office to see where he worked. Was that the crux of the matter—she had never cared enough?

Pushing open the door to the shop, he relegated all personal thoughts to a distant part of his mind. Ruminating over things that could not be changed was a waste of time. And Rand used his efficiently. Hadn't the few hours this morning on the phone with his office proved that?

"Rand!" Margot's face lit up when he walked in. For a moment he forgot his plans to ignore what couldn't be changed. Her look of delight hit him hard. Was she happy to show off her business, or was she truly glad to see him?

Ten minutes later he'd been given the grand tour. And was impressed. His little college dropout had built a successful business. The photos from the homes she'd decorated were impressive, as was her business acumen. Rand was proud of her.

And more convinced than ever they had no future together. She didn't need anything he had to offer. She'd gone on with her life, made a place for herself, established ties and roots.

He suggested lunch and Margot directed them to a small family restaurant that was obviously a favorite of hers. The hostess greeted her by name and showed them immediately to a choice patio table.

Shaded by a huge trellis of bougainvilleas, the patio setting was shaded with a small fountain in the back splashing merrily on rocks. An ornate cage of mourning doves to one side provided a melodious background.

Other businessmen and women were already seated at tables scattered around the patio. Rand noticed Margot fit right in.

Once they'd ordered, Margot turned to him, a certain eagerness in her eyes.

"Okay," she said. "What did you think?"

"I told you at the shop, you've done a magnificent job."

She sighed and smiled. "It's not a big venture like your company. But it's all mine."

"And you make a nice income, I take it?"

She nodded. It was nothing like what he probably earned, but it was suitable for her needs. And with the money now coming from her grandmother's estate, she would be able to expand. Maybe start a sideline of offering affordable decorating ideas for young couples who didn't have the money she currently demanded. With the higher priced assignments carrying the business, she could expand to offer a wider variety of services.

But she had to wait for her share of the estate.

"So tell me about starting up Designs by Margot," Rand suggested.

Margot complied, forgetting where she was, that others might be eavesdropping on her conversation. Her enthusiasm for her own business was strong, and she loved talking about it. Had their baby lived, she knew she would be a doting mother. With no child to pour her attention on, business had become her passion.

"I still think you should keep Beaufort Hall and use it as a showcase for your talents," Rand said at one point.

Margot's enthusiasm ended.

"No," she said abruptly. There were no warm feelings associated with the old house. She just wanted to be rid of it.

Stubborn, he thought in some surprise. Had she been so stubborn when they'd lived together? He didn't remember that.

Mostly what he remembered were her loving arms greeting him each night and her passionate kisses each morning, which almost compelled him to stay home with her all day and forget work.

And he remembered how happy she'd been when she'd discovered she was pregnant.

He'd wanted to give her the moon, and instead had only caused heartache.

"Tell me where your apartment is in relation to the shop," he said, pushing away the old memories. It was enough today to spend a few hours with her. Tonight he would end the idyllic visit, give her the papers to sign and return to New Orleans in the morning.

"It's a few blocks from here. If I don't need my car during the day, I usually walk to work."

"I'd like to see it."

"Why?"

"To satisfy my curiosity. Why else?"

"I don't know." Margot bit her lip in indecision. Then slowly nodded. "Okay, I guess we could walk over. I stopped by yesterday to get my mail, and air the place out a little. I've been staying at Beaufort Hall since Grandmother became ill.''

The street was lined with older homes and newer apartments. Lots of flowers added color to the neatly trimmed lawns. Margot's apartment building was an old house complete with a wide wooden porch and ornate double doors opening into a small foyer. One door left and right led to the ground-floor apartments. The steep stairs straight ahead gave access to the second-story apartments.

Margot unlocked the left door and entered. He stepped inside and stopped.

The warm colors hit him first. Soft yellow, a touch of tan and brown, blended with the predominant cream color. Plants were everywhere—colorful petunias in a window box; hanging plants in the corners; a small container of African violets on her table. The ceilings were high as was common with old Mississippi homes. The windows almost spanned the walls from the ceiling to the floor. The dark oak floors were polished to a high gloss.

For a poignant moment it reminded him of their apartment in New Orleans, though none of the furnishings looked familiar.

''Nice,'' he said. The room suited her. The furniture was comfortable and appealing. None of the cold formality of Beaufort Hall. He almost smiled—Harriet must have hated it.

"Thanks. Want something to drink?"

"Iced tea if you have it."

"I don't but it won't take long to make. Have a seat."

Rand took off his suit jacket and slung it over a chair. Ignoring Margot's invitation to sit, he wandered around the living room studying the paintings, the knickknacks that she had scattered around—a porcelain figure on a side table, a glass globe with a flower forever suspended inside on the bookshelves against the far wall. A framed picture of Margot with her sisters. He picked it up, remembering the day. Both Shelby and Georgia had come to New Orleans right after school that June. They'd all gone to the French Quarter, acting like tourists, eating at the Café du Monde, wandering through the Quarter. He'd snapped the shot with Georgia's camera.

They all looked so happy.

And so young.

Replacing it gently, he realized that was another aspect of Margot that was forever lost. The hint of sadness in her eyes, the pensive moods she sometimes fell into, all changes the years and circumstances had wrought. She no longer looked young and carefree.

He turned and headed for her minuscule

kitchen, pausing in the doorway. A table and single chair stood beneath a window that overlooked the side yard. Counter space was practically nonexistent. Even the appliances looked like miniature versions of the real thing.

The teakettle started to hiss.

"Need help?"

She jumped and turned to glare at him. "Stop sneaking up on me."

"I walked in, no sneaking," he said calmly. Folding his arms across his chest, he leaned against the jamb.

Margot eyed him suspiciously. A quiet Rand was a dangerous Rand. What did he want now?

Waiting for the teakettle to boil, she had already put the tea bags in the teapot and taken out the ice. She'd let the tea steep, then poured it into a plastic container full of ice. That would cool it enough to pour it into glasses. Normally she kept a pitcher in the refrigerator, but hadn't been home enough recently.

She should say something, but after lunch, after discussing her company and her plans, there wasn't much left to say.

And that made her sad. Once she and Rand had thought they'd never run out of words. Now he seemed like a stranger.

Idly she noticed her answering machine

blinking. For something to do, she reached over and hit the button.

"Hi, Margot, Susan here. Haven't heard from you in a while, kiddo. I'll try the Hall."

A beep, then Susan's voice again. "You're a hard woman to track down. Caroline said you went into work. Your assistant said you went to lunch. So in hopes you check your messages, give me a call. I want to see how you're doing."

Another beep, then a strong masculine voice, came on,

"Margot? Philip here. How are you? I've tried calling a few times, but seem to miss you every time. I am happy to offer my services if you need any help with the estate. Do give me a call."

Another beep, then silence.

"Who is Philip?" Rand asked.

Margot looked at him in some surprise. "A friend."

He stepped closer and unfolded his arms.

"How good a friend?"

"I don't know. How do you classify friends?"

"By whether they come over to your place."

"And that would make a friend a good one?" she asked. "Susan comes over all the time."

"Is that Susan Carmody?" he asked.

She nodded. "Though she's married now and it's Susan Andrews. But yes. I'm surprised you remembered her."

"You and she were friends since first grade, why wouldn't I remember that?"

"You only met her once. We weren't married long enough for us to spend much time with any of my friends."

"Who is Philip?" he asked again. "Is he another good friend? Someone else who comes over here often? Maybe even stays the night?" A hard edge colored his voice.

She shook her head, her own temper beginning to flare. "Not that it's any of your business, but no, Philip has never come over—even for dinner—much less to stay the night!"

"It's my business until you sign those papers," he said, reaching out to cradle her head in his large hands. "Until then, you are still my wife." Lowering his face he started to kiss her, but Margot pulled away.

"Stop, Rand. What we had is over. I can have whomever I wish to have as a friend. Did you think I lived in a vacuum since you've been gone?"

"Who left who, sweet?" he asked, a dangerous glint in his eyes.

She took a breath and nodded her head. "Okay, so maybe technically I left you. And with Grandmother's interference we never got back together. But I wrote you. About six months later I did write."

She sighed and bit her lower lip. "I guess Grandmother interfered. I take it the letter never reached you?"

He shook his head. "Why didn't you just come to New Orleans?" he asked.

"Because I hadn't heard anything from you and I thought you didn't care. I needed to have some sign of what to do next. By then I couldn't stay at the Hall any longer. She was driving me crazy. Shelby had found a job in New Orleans and Georgia graduated from high school and seemed set on nursing. I wanted some plan in my life, some goal or purpose. The plans we made were in ashes. So I thought if we talked—I don't know, maybe I could get a clue about what I needed to do with the rest of my life."

"I never got the letter," he said.

"I guessed as much when we figured out Harriet had intercepted yours. At the time she said it was just further proof that you really had no use for me and I should cut my losses. She sounded sympathetic. Now of course I know it for the lie it was."

"So I'm here now. We're face-to-face. Maybe it's time to talk things out. See what we want to do from this point forward."

"I thought you wanted to split up!"

"I need to change the status quo, Margot. Either end the marriage, or resume it."

She stared at him. He'd voiced what she'd been thinking about for days!

But there was no mention of any feelings. Why the sudden change of heart?

"Resume it? But we've just agreed to a divorce!"

"It's been at the back of my mind since we made love—and I think we should at least discuss it."

"I have my business here, you live hours away in New Orleans where your company is. I don't see how that would ever work."

"I didn't say it will work, necessarily. But it is an option to consider. Or we can continue with the divorce proceedings."

He said it as if either choice held the same appeal. Which would he prefer? she wondered.

"I don't know." Margot glanced around. She had built a life for herself. Did she wish to change things? Wish to open herself up to the uncertainty of living with Rand again?

How about the excitement of living with him? a small voice whispered.

"Come this weekend and see how you like New Orleans. It's been a while since you were there," he suggested.

"Five years. I've never been back."

"Come for the weekend. At the very least you can give me some pointers on my apartment. It doesn't give the welcoming warmth that yours conveys. Think of it as an assignment—I can be a new client."

Margot was tempted. What would one weekend hurt? Especially if it led to a reconciliation? No, not a reconciliation—not in the truest sense of the word. Just a resumption of their marriage.

Maybe seeing Rand in his own space, seeing how he lived today would help her with this endless fascination she had about the man.

"I can't come this weekend. I have a client who is flying in from New York. We've set up this appointment a couple of months ago. I put her off once because of Harriet's illness. I don't want to do it again or I risk losing the assignment."

"Next weekend, then."

Feeling a curl of anticipation, Margot slowly nodded. "Okay, next weekend."

"Come on Friday."

"If I can get away."

"The advantages of owning your own business, you're the boss."

"As are you."

He nodded.

"I expect you to be there when I'm there,

Rand. Not working late, no dashing off for a quick minute on Saturday.''

Slowly he smiled, his eyes warming as he gazed down into hers. Margot felt her heart turned somersaults.

No other man had ever fascinated her as Rand had. Nor had any enticed her beyond a friendly meal or a visit to the local movie theater. Rand had outright spoiled her for other men. His smile had the power to melt her bones, his touch wreaked havoc with her senses and his voice could charm the birds from the trees. But would he believe her if she told him?

"If we are even beginning to explore resuming our marriage, I don't think you should be seeing anyone else," he said.

"I'm not seeing anyone," she replied, pouring tea over ice, and holding out a glass for him.

He glanced at the answering machine.

"Philip was a friend of my grandmother's. He's in his fifties. I hardly think you need to feel any competition with him," she said dryly. After five years, no matter what they planned to try in the future, Rand had lost some of his rights to tell her who to see.

Rand drained the glass, placing it on the counter.

"I have to be heading out, Margot. I want to

be back in the office this afternoon before it closes. See you a week from Friday.''

He was almost to the living room before she could speak.

''Wait! What do you mean? You're leaving now?'' She followed him, watching in disbelief as he picked up his jacket.

''I have work to do.'' His hand on the doorknob, he looked at her. ''If you can get there by lunchtime, let me know. We'll have lunch together. Otherwise, I'll plan on dinner next Friday.''

''I don't know where you live or work,'' she said, trying to prolong his stay. His leaving caught her totally unaware.

Reaching into his inside jacket pocket he withdrew a card and turned to hand it to her, careful to keep his fingers from touching her.

Margot looked at it and then Rand. What was going on? He'd invited her to visit and once she said yes, he couldn't get away fast enough.

What about his suggestion they consider trying again?

''I'll see you a week from Friday.'' He left before she could say another word.

She ran to the window and watched him stride down the street, his suit jacket slung over one shoulder, his long legs making short work of the block. In moments, he'd turned the corner and was lost from sight.

"Blast it!" She slapped her hand against the wall beside the window. The man was the most confusing person she knew. And the most infuriating. She had thought he'd spend the week. Stupid of her to assume that. He'd never said how long he planned to stay.

Leaning her forehead against the glass, she already missed him.

The next morning Margot dressed conservatively for her meeting with the attorney. She hadn't told Rand about the appointment. Of course she had other things to think about. Mostly how she felt about him, and if being with him a few hours here and there were enough to consider his suggestion of resuming their marriage.

She would have liked something a bit more romantic, something to give her an indication of how he felt about things—especially as it hadn't been that long since they'd been agreeing to a divorce. She'd lost so much more than a baby and husband five years ago. She'd lost the ability to believe in happy-ever-after, to believe love lasted.

She paused on her way out of the old mansion to glare at Harriet's portrait over the mantel in the living room. She knew now that Rand had not been the irresponsible uninterested man Harriet had made him out to be. He had tried to contact her, but Harriet had interfered.

More than ever Margot wanted to find out about her father. Just something to give her the closure she needed. Just to know he'd not willingly walked away from his wife and daughters would make a world of difference to her.

Time enough later to dwell on that. Right now she had to hurry or risk being late.

An hour and a half later Margot stepped outside the lawyer's office into the sunlight, shocked. Being late would have been the least of her problems, she thought as she checked her watch.

She began walking slowly back to her car, feeling totally confused. There was almost too much to comprehend, she thought dazed. Too much to calmly return to work and act as if her entire world had not been turned upside down yet again.

She tossed the thick envelope with the copies of the papers the attorney had reviewed onto the front seat. She had to tell Shelby and Georgia. They were both counting on money from the estate. How would they react when she told them there was nothing but debts? She needed to see them in person; this was not something she wanted to share over the phone.

They could meet when she went to New Orleans. She'd call and tell them she was coming and arrange a convenient time.

Leaning her head against her seat back, she closed her eyes. Tired beyond belief, she wished fervently for an end to it all. The revelations kept coming and coming and she wasn't sure she was up to dealing with them. Opening her eyes, she took a deep breath. She'd just have to be.

But she wasn't looking forward to telling her sisters there was no money. Just thinking about explaining how Harriet had incurred monumental debts just to keep that monstrous house of hers going infuriated her.

She sure didn't want Rand finding out. Not yet anyway.

She had enough to deal with concerning his sudden suggestion they resume their marriage. What was she going to do about that?

CHAPTER EIGHT

THE week dragged by for Margot. After meeting with her long postponed appointment at the weekend, she wished she had canceled again and gone instead to New Orleans. The woman could not decide on a basic color scheme, much less what she wanted for decor and furnishings. She had just bought an elegant old home in Natchez and wanted to furnish it appropriately. That was all she'd say.

Margot held onto her patience by a thread. She wanted to scream at the woman that she had more important matters to concern herself with and once she had made up her mind to call.

Instead she remained silent, patiently showing different designs, offering new suggestions.

But all the way back to Beaufort Hall, she fumed. She could have been in New Orleans. Rand and she could be going to dinner at Paul K's or The Aubergine. She could have already shared the burden of the lawyer's news with her sisters.

Instead she still had more papers to read

through in an attempt to prove her grandmother had been instrumental in driving their father away. She wondered how much more she needed. After learning what Harriet had done with her own marriage, she no longer had any doubts about her parents' breakup.

The phone rang around eight. She hurried into the hall to answer, thinking if she owned the house the first thing she would have done was make sure every room had a phone extension.

"Hello?"

"Margot? It's Rand."

Foolishly a grin started on her face. Her heart swelled. He'd called! She gripped the receiver tightly, wishing she could have seen him, been with him.

"Hi. What's up?"

"Just called to say I wish you had come down this weekend."

"Me, too."

"How did your meeting with your client go?"

"It was a total bust. Honestly, the woman hasn't a clue what she wants. I think she expected me to show her everything there is in the world. She'll know what she wants when she sees it."

"So did you?"

"No, I showed her general groupings and left her with some samples and color combinations to think about. We'll meet again on Wednesday."

Maybe by then she wouldn't feel so restless, so incomplete. Maybe she would be able to stop thinking constantly about Rand and be able to focus on her job! And by Wednesday, she had only two more days before she'd see Rand again.

"You never told me the outcome of the situation when your tanker ran aground," she said, longing to prolong her connection. She wanted to learn all she could about Rand, what he'd been doing for the last five years, what his life was like now.

"We had it in to be examined, looks fine. It ran aground on a sandbar, no rocks. It's been recertified and is back in service."

"That's good. Do accidents like that happen often?" she asked.

"Thankfully, no."

"Tell me more about the shipping industry," she said, sinking to the floor beside the phone. Anxious to keep Rand on the line, to drive away the loneliness of the day, she grasped at any straw.

"When you come to visit. How are you doing

getting through your grandmother's papers?" he asked.

"I've read everything up to seven years ago. It's going fast now. I doubt there'll be any mention of it after all this time. I did find an envelope with my mother's death certificate and each of our birth certificates."

"Did you know when your mother died?"

"Yes. We've visited her grave, read the dates on the tombstone. It was funny to see the birth certificates, though. Sam Williams is our father's name, you know. But we've always used Beaufort," she said slowly.

"How did that happen?"

"Apparently Mama took it back after he left. I don't even remember being called Williams, but then I was so little when it all happened. I haven't found anything to show that it was legally changed—my name and Shelby's and Georgia's. Do you suppose that makes our marriage illegal?"

"No, it doesn't." His tone was sharp, forceful.

"It might be a moot point, I guess."

"Because?"

"If we decide to divorce."

"We'll talk about that next weekend. What time are you coming?"

"I'll try to be there for lunch."

"I'll arrange to be free."

"Um, Rand, I need to meet my sisters for lunch on Saturday. It's the only time Georgia had free. So, if you have something to do then—" She hated to bring up the lunch, but after making such a point of wanting him to spend time with her exclusively, she needed to let him know she couldn't reciprocate.

"Not invited, eh?"

How could she tactfully explain? She wouldn't invite him even if she didn't have bad news to share. She didn't want to give rise to any speculation from her sisters before she decided what she wanted to do.

"It's a girls' lunch."

"Save dinner for me."

"I will."

She hung up, still unsure of her feelings. Impatient to see him again, reluctant to be drawn into his circle of influence, she wasn't sure what she expected, or wanted. Only, she was sure she'd go through with the visit. She had to know what the future might hold.

By Friday, Margot was a nervous wreck. She had packed and unpacked four times, trying to choose just the right clothes to take. She wanted to show Rand how far she'd come from the shy young college girl who had rebelled against her formal, regal grandmother. Her casual clothes now carried the look of distinction. No more jeans with the knees torn. Instead she had slacks and shirts that fit her slender frame and displayed her womanly attributes. Discreet jewelry. For dinner, she'd chosen a silk jumpsuit in dark blue. With a plunging neckline and close-fitting bodice, it also made her feel very sexy.

Sexy? She shook her head. She had no reason to be sexy. She and Rand needed to sit down and have a frank discussion about what they each wanted, what they each expected if they resumed their marriage.

Then she could feel sexy, an imp inside insisted, for those memory-making times Rand seemed to excel in.

By late Friday morning, the closer she drove toward New Orleans, the more her emotions began to change. Trepidation filled her. She wanted to see Rand, and her sisters, but was she ready to face New Orleans? She had been so happy there, and so devastated. Memories sprang to mind, lingered. The university, nights studying while Rand worked beside her. Decorating their apartment on a shoestring budget. The walks she and Rand took along the Mississippi. Shopping for Christmas gifts. They'd only had one Christmas together. And five apart.

Finally she let the memories of their excitement over the baby come to mind. She'd been thrilled about their coming child. As had Rand.

Once again, she savored the memory of his pleasure in the first teddy bear, bought right after they had confirmation she was pregnant. He'd wanted to buy a football, but she'd asked him to wait until they at least knew if the baby was a boy or not.

She remembered what he said about turning to work to fill the emptiness left by the loss. She'd been too young to articulate her needs. She had expected him to intuitively know she ached with sorrow and make things better for her. But she'd never realized he'd felt the same way. That he'd needed comfort and reassurance, too.

Was she more mature now? Could she deal better with the vagaries of fate in the future because of the past? She sure hoped so. She was fighting for her marriage in the only way she knew.

The traffic grew heavier, occupying her attention. The old memories were once again relegated to another time.

Weaving around the area near Canal Street, she located the high-rise in which Rand's company was housed. Parking was a problem, but she finally found a spot. Checking her watch, she saw it was not quite noon.

She entered the cavernous lobby and located the bank of phones. Pulling out Rand's card, she dialed.

By the time she got through, she was almost giddy with excitement.

"Where are you?" he asked once she'd identified herself.

"Downstairs."

"Want to come up and see the place, or are you ready for lunch now?" he asked.

"I want to see it."

"Come up to the eleventh floor."

In only minutes she stepped into the tastefully decorated lobby of The Blue Star Shipping Company.

"May I help you?" The receptionist behind the desk was blond, young and a perfect fit for the surroundings.

"I'm here to see Rand Marstall," Margot said with a smile.

"Is he expecting you?" The haughty tone of the receptionist's voice rubbed Margot the wrong way. She stopped smiling.

"Yes."

"Whom shall I say?"

"His wife." She couldn't help the pride in her voice.

Margot had not said the words aloud in years. But suddenly they felt right. Was she already committed to making an attempt to resume their marriage? Or was it for the sheer pleasure of seeing the woman's eyes widen, her expression change.

Before the receptionist could notify Rand, he strode into the lobby from the hall to the left.

"Margot," he said.

An imp of mischief, spurred from the receptionist's surprise, had Margot reach up and offer a kiss.

"Hello, darling."

"I see you got here safely," he said, not by a flicker of his expression showing any surprise at her greeting.

She tucked her hand into his arm and smiled up at him. "Of course, though I'd forgotten how awful the traffic is in this city. Going to show me around?"

He nodded and started back down the hall.

"Care to share with me what game you're playing now?" he asked once they were out of the reception area.

She looked up at him with feigned innocence. "Why, Rand, no games. Can't a wife greet her husband?"

"Right." He walked straight through his secretary's area without saying a word—even when the woman looked up expectantly. Pulling Margot into his office, he shut the door, leaned against it and pulled her into his arms. His kiss was all she remembered: hot, exciting, seductive—the stuff of dreams.

Forgetting everything but the pleasure his touch brought, she leaned into the kiss, opening her mouth. Would they skip lunch and make a new memory?

Rand felt her acquiescence and deepened the kiss. He abhorred games and wanted to teach her a lesson, but one touch of her mouth against his and he forgot everything except the feel of Margot in his arms. Her sexy body was pressed against his, he could feel the soft curves and delectable valleys. Her arms were tight around his neck and she returned his kiss fervently.

When he finally eased away to look down at her, she raised her lids and gazed back. He noted she was breathless and smiled suddenly. He'd like to keep her that way. But was he opening himself up for further heartache? He had his life as he wanted it. Work was compelling and satisfying. He had a small circle of friends to spend leisure time with. When he remembered to take it.

Yet he had missed this woman like no one else in his life. His attorney thought him a fool to pursue this chancy arrangement, but he was in for the long haul—to see what they could salvage, if anything, from their earlier marriage.

"Wow," she said, a smile lighting her eyes. "Another memory?"

He looked ruefully around his office. Another memory? One he'd regret if they didn't resume their marriage. His office had been safe from reminders of Margot before this. Now—

"Ready for lunch?" he asked, putting her a step away from him. He was ready for a lot more than eating, but knew the value of patience in delicate negotiations.

So much had changed in the last few weeks, he could afford to wait and see what developed. If things were not going the way he wanted, he'd take a different tactic at that juncture.

"Yes, I'm hungry," she said. She'd not been able to eat breakfast for the excitement. Now she felt as if she could eat a horse. "But show me around first."

"On the way out," he promised. "I'll introduce you to Betty Jean, my secretary, first."

"Are you free the rest of the day?"

"Yes." He crossed to the desk and closed a folder, tidied a stack of papers. Looking up at her, he winked.

"Free all weekend. We'll do whatever a tourist to New Orleans likes."

"I'm hardly a tourist, I lived here for a

while,'' she said, walking over to the window
to look out at the view. His office was near
Canal Street, and not too far from the Quarter.
Beyond the French Quarter she could see the
wide Mississippi River. Container ships were
inching by the Crescent City, on their way to
sea. It felt strange to be back.

"Where are you parked?'' Rand asked.

"About two blocks over. I'll have to move
the car. It's in a two-hour limit."

"Give me a description and the keys, I'll
have someone drive it to my place."

She smiled and reached into her purse for the
keys. Things *had* changed. What an extravagance.

"And how will that person return to work?''

"Get a cab, take the bus. How should I
know?'' he asked impatiently.

She nodded. Definitely a change. Was he
happy with the success he'd made? she wondered.

He gave her a whirlwind tour of the office,
introducing her to managers and clerks, secre-
taries and analysts. Her head was swimming,
but the tour gave her a new appreciation for
how far her husband had come. Wistfully she
wished she could have shared that climb with
him.

They ate lunch at a small bistro off Canal

Street, then Rand suggested they change their clothes before prowling around the Quarter.

He flagged a cab and in only moments they were in the renovated district near the River. The old warehouses had been converted to expensive apartments and condominiums. He opened the door to his building and escorted Margot to the elevator, wondering what she'd think about his place. It was a far cry from their little apartment near the university.

He opened the door and stood aside for her to enter, wishing he was privy to her thoughts when she saw it.

Margot stepped inside and looked around. Sleek, sophisticated and cold were the first three adjectives that came to mind. Dismayed, she kept walking into the room, afraid to let Rand see her expression. Was this the kind of home he liked? He must have hated their place with the vibrant colors and clutter. She liked pillows and plants and pictures and color above all. This room looked like a museum, or showcase room.

"It's lovely," she said when the silence stretched out awkwardly. She spotted her suitcases with her keys on top. "If you tell me where to change, I'll only be a minute."

He closed the door and walked over, turning her around and raising her face with a finger.

"Where do you want to stay, Margot? My room or the guest room?"

She frowned, wishing he'd made that decision.

"The guest room," she said at last. Nothing had been settled. She needed the distance and space before committing herself. There was still so much to decide. And so much to work through before she'd feel truly comfortable around Rand. If she ever did.

If he were disappointed, he hid it well. Lifting her bags, he led the way. "Follow me" was all he said.

Alone a few seconds later, Margot unpacked and surveyed the clothes she'd brought. Deciding on a casual skirt and lacy top, she quickly changed. It was cool, which she'd need in this unusually early heat and humidity. Brushing her hair, she checked in the mirror. Ready as I'll ever be, she thought.

When she walked into the living room Rand stood by the window, talking on the phone. He turned and beckoned her over.

"I can be there for a while tomorrow, one o'clock. But I won't stay long."

Margot stepped into his arm as naturally as if she'd been doing it for years, instead of having a long gap when they'd been apart. She breathed in his subtle scent, looking out across the Mississippi, and wondering if she was doing the right thing by coming. She refused to allow her doubts to take hold.

He hung up the phone and kissed her cheek gently. ''All set?''

''Business again?'' she asked.

''Right. But this weekend is for you. Since you're having lunch tomorrow with your sisters, I'll meet with Patterson then, and be free by the time you are.''

''Fair enough. Where to first?''

''Jax?''

''Good starting place. You must think I really am a tourist.'' The converted brewery was now comprised of trendy shops and tourist attractions that beckoned at the entrance to the Vieux Carré.

''Sturdy walking shoes?'' he asked, checking.

''Comfortable and enduring.''

He took her hand, threading his fingers through hers. ''Let's go play tourist.''

Margot's memories again mingled with the present, remembering Rand's likes and dislikes as easily as she knew her own. They had often walked around the French Quarter when younger, an inexpensive way to spend a lazy Sunday, or to hunt bargains for their apartment.

Sometimes it seemed as if they'd never been apart.

Other times, Rand seemed like a stranger.

It was disconcerting, but Margot was determined to explore all facets of the man beside her. This weekend could be the most important one of her life.

They wandered around the old French Quarter, stopped in shops, watched sidewalk artists sketch other tourists. Refusing a carriage ride, they darted across the street from Jackson Square to snack on beignets and café au lait.

They ate at a Cajun place on a side street, then walked back through the twilight to Rand's apartment.

When Rand switched on the light in the living room, he looked around and frowned. This place did not welcome anyone. Whatever they decided about their future, he wanted Margot to do something with his home.

"What do you think about the apartment?" he asked.

"I told you it's lovely."

"It's not like our place was. When I first got it, I wanted something very different. Now, I don't know." He shook his head and headed for the kitchen.

"Want something to drink?"

"Iced tea." She looked at the room from a

professional perspective. "It needs some color," she called. She wanted to see the rest of the apartment. Following him into the kitchen, she noted the stainless-steel appliances, the austere counter space. "It also doesn't look as if anyone lives here," she said slowly.

Rand shrugged. "I've lived here for years. Had a professional design the place."

He looked up from pouring iced tea from a pitcher and caught her eye. "Want to have a go at it?"

"What would you like?"

"You decorate it, Margot. Whatever you like, I'm sure will suit me."

She nodded, ideas already crowding her mind on how to change the austere look into one of warmth and comfort—without making too many alterations.

They drank iced tea sitting side by side on the easy chairs that faced the wide windows, watching the night lights across the river, and the slowly moving lights on the riverboats. It was peaceful, Margot realized a few minutes later. They talked generally about New Orleans, how the Saints were doing, reclamation projects dredging the river and the changes in the Quarter.

When it was completely dark, Rand took her

glass and put it on the table beside his, pulling her into his lap.

"Time to talk about us, Margot," he said.

She lay against his chest, her eyes still fixed on the darkness outside the apartment. He had not turned on any lights, so they were cocooned in the night. Only the lights outside offering a break in the velvety black. She was silent for a long moment, relishing being with Rand, feeling quietly content for the first time in years.

"I missed you this week," she said slowly, willing to admit that much, but not more until she had a better feeling of how Rand felt. Or where this conversation was heading.

"That's encouraging," he said dryly.

"I was looking for something more than that in return," she said with spirit.

"What, that I missed you, too? Take it as a given."

"You could have called."

"I did last week, remember?"

"And the phone lines were down after that?"

"They work both ways, Margot. You could have called me."

He was right. If they were serious about trying again, she needed to do more than sit back and let him pursue her. She'd grown up during the last few years. Everything didn't come automatically. Marriage needed to be a partnership, with both partners contributing equally.

"You're right, I should have," she said. "Especially Wednesday when I really needed to talk to someone—" She stopped abruptly, remembering she didn't want to tell Rand just yet about the news she'd received from the attorney. Time enough once she and her sisters had decided on a plan. For now, she'd do her best to keep the weekend pleasant.

"If we decide to resume the marriage, I think we need to discuss ground rules. Make sure our expectations are laid out so there are no surprises, and no disappointments."

Margot realized he'd said nothing about love. Where did that come into the equation? Or had he lost what love he felt for her? Was this just expedient?

"What would you expect?" she asked, almost afraid to hear what he had to say.

His hand rubbed against her arm, his fingers tracing light patterns against her skin. The erotic distraction caused Margot to focus harder on the conversation. For a moment, she wanted to deny the need for a discussion, turn in his arms and kiss him, have passion take over and block all thoughts and feelings and uncertainties that churned within her. But Rand was right. If they wanted a chance at living together again, they had to be clear about what they expected.

"I'd want to live together," he said.

She nodded, her head brushing against his. "Of course."

"Does that prove a problem with your business? You couldn't commute to Natchez."

She'd been thinking about that all week. "I plan to leave Jessie in charge, make her a partner. Then I could open another branch here in New Orleans." It would be hard to leave the clients she'd developed, harder than ever to start up a business in New Orleans. More costly, more competition. But she could at least make the attempt.

"I can help you, if you like,"

"I'll see. For now I'd like to try it on my own," she said. "What about you, will you have to work as long each day now that you've built up your company?" she asked. There had to be concessions on both sides for this to work.

"I won't kid you, Margot, there are a lot of demands on my time. But I'll curtail some of them, find someone else who can handle the workload. I'll do my best to be home for dinner every night and on the weekends."

"What else?" she asked.

"Children."

She drew in a sharp breath.

"I don't think so, Rand. I don't want to go through that again. I couldn't bear it." Tears threatened. Just thinking about how happy they'd been and then the sudden loss was almost more than she could think about.

"We both wanted children before," he said softly. "I still want them. One or two. Someone to leave all that I've built to. You'd make an excellent mother."

"No, Rand." Struggling to sit up, Margot pushed out of his lap and moved to the window, leaning against the cool pane. "If that's one of your conditions to resuming this marriage, then we'd better call a halt now. I can't go through that again."

"Another pregnancy doesn't mean you'll miscarry."

"But I could. I could," she whispered, feeling the familiar ache taking over. She had yearned for her baby so much, been crushed when she miscarried. She wasn't strong enough to face that twice in one lifetime.

CHAPTER NINE

MARGOT awoke early the next morning to the aroma of freshly brewing coffee. She turned over in the guest bed and gazed around the room. The decor cried out for as much attention as the living room did. Almost snow-white—everything went together perfectly, yet had no color, no personality, no soul. She wondered who the interior decorator had been. Maybe there was a call for her business here after all.

Stretching slowly, Margot sat up in bed, the lacy confection of her gown wasted, she thought ruefully, by her sleeping alone. But Rand had not swept her away and after the discussion last night it seemed as if they were further from resolving their situation that ever. He wanted children. She couldn't risk it without a built-in guarantee, which she knew life didn't give.

Sighing softly, she worried she'd made a mistake in coming, in listening to Rand's tantalizing suggestion. Could they resume their marriage? Would things work out as they'd once planned?

She pushed away the sheets and rose. The sky was clear blue, the sun just peeping over the horizon. She had lots of time before meeting her sisters. Taking a quick shower, she donned one of the lightweight dresses she'd brought. Sandals on her feet would suffice. She didn't plan on a long walking tour today. And she was anxious to see Rand. To talk with him, spend time together and see what resulted.

When she entered the kitchen, Rand sat at the breakfast nook reading a paper, a half full cup of coffee before him on the table. It looked so ordinary. But the rapid increase in her heart rate wasn't ordinary—except around Rand. For a moment, Margot wanted to throw herself into his arms and let his kisses consume her. Let his touch chase away the doubts and uncertainties that seemed stronger than ever.

Instead she smiled shyly, and said, ''Good morning.''

Would he be angry she had elected to spend the night alone?

He looked up, his eyes gleaming at the sight of her.

''Sleep well?'' he asked.

She shrugged. ''Not particularly, but not because of the bed.''

''Because you really wanted to be in with me,

right?'' he asked, rising to fetch another cup and pour her coffee.

She wondered how long she could avoid answering that loaded question.

He tilted her face up to his on the way back to the table and brushed his lips across hers. ''Well?'' he asked, his eyes dancing in amusement.

''Maybe we should have made another memory last night,'' she admitted grudgingly. She had to be honest if they were to make changes.

He almost laughed. ''No maybe about it. But we have time. In the interim, what would you like for breakfast?''

''You're going to fix it?'' she asked.

''I will if you want, but was rather hoping you'd insist on doing the honors. It's been years since I enjoyed your cooking.''

''I could make an omelet,'' she offered. She remembered how he liked his. In fact, Margot realized, she remembered everything about Rand—the Rand she used to know and love.

But the love she'd once known seemed to grow with each passing day. Startled to finally admit she loved him, she moved away, lest she blurt it out. He had made no allusion to love even when suggesting they resume their marriage—just offered a renewed partnership. Was a half loaf better than none? If they resumed their relationship, would he come to fall in love with her again, or had her desertion put paid to that for all time?

She wasn't sure she could agree to such a one-sided arrangement. She wanted to be loved.

"If I cook today, are you cooking tomorrow?" she asked, opening cupboard doors hunting bowls and pans.

"Nope, I thought tomorrow morning we'd get the Sunday *Picayune* and head for Café du Monde where we can sip café au lait and while away the morning reading the paper."

She smiled. That had been almost a tradition for them each Sunday. She thought their brief stop there yesterday afternoon had been for old time's sake. Now she was touched that he remembered that ritual, and seemed to be doing his best to recapture the pleasant aspects of their life together.

Only on the question of children were they at different ends of the spectrum.

"When and where are you meeting Georgia and Shelby?" Rand asked as they ate.

His appreciation of her cooking was gratifying. She rarely cooked anymore. As she'd told him weeks ago, cooking for one wasn't as much fun as cooking for Rand. Watching him eat with such relish made it all worthwhile.

"Court of the Two Sisters at twelve-thirty."

She'd chosen that restaurant because of the wide spacing of tables. They'd be assured a certain amount of privacy while talking. They could have met at Shelby's apartment, but Margot wanted to treat her sisters to lunch. As a kind of celebration of her possible return to New Orleans.

"I'll drop you off on my way to the office. I can pick you up later, if you like," he said easily.

"Not necessary. One of my sisters can drop me back here. Or I'll get a cab."

Rand rose and left, returning in only a moment. "Here. If you get back before I do." He held out a key. By its shiny condition, it looked new.

Margot stared at it for a long moment. Should she accept?

He took her hand, dropped the key in her palm and closed her fingers over it. His warm hand engulfed hers. The sensations caused by his touch chased up her arm, through her body until Margot felt enveloped by his touch. She looked up, a question in her eyes.

"No strings," he said.

Did he read minds now? she wondered. When they lived together, he had seemed completely baffled by her behavior many times. That came from both of them being so young, she thought, so young and untried. Now he seemed to understand her. Or was that wishful thinking?

Nodding, she slipped the key into her pocket. "I won't lose it."

"Have you thought about redecorating this place?" he asked as he resumed his seat.

Hesitantly at first, then with more conviction, Margot capsulized her ideas for the different rooms she'd seen. By primarily using accessories in bold colors, and a few additional pieces of furniture, she could make the apartment into a warm and beautiful home.

Rand rocked back on the rear legs of his chair, hands in the pockets. He watched her through narrowed eyes, nodding from time to time. "Sounds like a plan. Run with it," he said at last.

"I haven't seen the entire apartment."

"Then come on. I'll show you every nook and cranny."

Leaving the dishes on the table, Margot rose and followed Rand. She'd seen the guest room; it was only his bedroom and bath she'd not yet seen. He walked into the huge room and turned, resting his hands on her shoulders.

"My bedroom." He lowered his head and kissed her lightly. "Our room?" he asked softly.

She swallowed, and turned to study the room, intrigued by the huge bed that dominated the room. The dark spread and navy sheets and blankets looked functional and masculine. She had flower-covered sheets and a comforter with lots of ruffles on her bed. The contrast was interesting to say the least. Somehow she couldn't envision Rand sleeping on ruffly, flowered, pastel sheets.

"What do you think?" he asked. Was there a hint of impatience in his tone?

"This is the best room in the house," she said. "It's got your stamp on it. The rest of the place looks like no one is at home."

Books were stacked on the bedside table. Change and keys littered the dresser. A large framed photograph of his parents stood in a prominent place.

She looked quickly away.

What had she expected? That he'd have a picture of her in his room? As far as he'd known, she'd deserted him, relaying the message that she never wanted to see him again. He'd moved on.

Anger at her grandmother boiled anew. Margot wished she'd suspected earlier. So much time wasted.

"Well?"

"Off the top of my head, you don't need to

do anything in here," she said. "This room fits you."

"How about us?"

"We'll see."

"Would you be comfortable sleeping in here?"

Heat washed through her. Sleeping and waking up with Rand every day? Having him kiss her, touch her, make love to her in that bed? She almost trembled with sudden longing.

She should not have left five years ago. She should not have stayed away once the worst of her pain had faded. *She* had failed their marriage, not Rand. The reality was proving almost harder to live with than she could manage.

Slowly, as if reading her mind again, Rand turned her around and locked her in his arms.

"Want to test the bed?" he asked in a husky voice.

Before she could respond, he lowered his head and kissed her.

Margot was late arriving at the Court of the Two Sisters. Both Georgia and Shelby were waiting at a table near the courtyard. She hurried to join them.

"Sorry. Have you been here long?" she asked, slipping into the empty chair.

"No." Georgia said, looking critically at her

older sister. She exchanged glances with Shelby. "What have you been up to?" she asked suspiciously.

Margot blushed and both her sisters grinned.

"As if we didn't know," Shelby said.

"Staying with Rand, right?" Georgia asked.

Margot picked up her menu and opened it, nodding once in response, trying to hide from their knowing eyes.

Shelby reached out and pushed the menu down. "So what is up? Are the two of you going to become an item again? Or is this just a weekend fling?"

"You don't have flings with your husband," Margot said primly, wishing she knew how to answer her sister. There was so much to decide. And it all seemed to rest with her.

"It could be when you haven't seen him in five years. What's the scoop?"

She hesitated, then shrugged. They'd find out soon enough.

"Actually, after spending a few days together at Beaufort Hall, we've sort of discussed seeing if we can pick up the threads of our marriage."

"Is this why we're here? To celebrate some momentous change in your life-style?" Georgia asked. "I bet the wife of Rand Marstall will eat here frequently."

Margot shook her head. "Nothing's been decided. Actually, when Rand came to see me a few weeks ago, it was to ask for a divorce.''

"Divorce!" Shelby said.

"Yes."

"Why? After all these years?"

"He can't have found someone new if you are discussing resuming your marriage," Georgia said shrewdly.

"No, it was just—closure, I guess you'd say. To do something to change the status quo after so many years.''

"How are you doing visiting here?" Shelby asked. Both her sisters knew how she equated New Orleans with the saddest time of her life.

"It is getting better, isn't it?" Georgia asked.

Margot nodded. "Tolerable, I guess." She tried to smile. The old ache would always be with her, but it was getting easier to go on.

"If you do get back with Rand, you should have another baby right away," Georgia said, opening her menu.

"No." Margot said sharply. "I don't want to go through that again."

Both women stared at her in surprise.

"But, Margot, just because you had one miscarriage, doesn't mean you'll have another one. I bet you and Rand would produce some wonderful children. I remember how excited you were when you discovered you were pregnant before. I can't imagine you not wanting a baby."

"I can't take the chance. Not ever," she said slowly. She could tell from the look on their faces they didn't understand. Maybe only another woman who had lived through such heartache would understand. But she knew she didn't have it in her to try again. Yes, she might carry a baby to term, but she could also lose it and that she couldn't bear.

"But that's not why I wanted to see you for lunch. Rand and I will have to decide what we want to do with our future. When we do, you two will be the first to know. But in the meantime, I have bad news about Harriet's estate."

The waitress chose that moment to appear to take their orders. When she was gone, Shelby turned to Margot. "Okay, give. What's wrong?"

"There's no money," Margot said bluntly.

"What?" Georgia asked in disbelief. "There has to be. Grandmother lived lavishly. She belonged to the country club, had that huge old home with lots of servants, dressed to the nines."

Margot nodded. "All on borrowed money. It turns out she made some bad investments a number of years ago. She mortgaged Beaufort Hall, then made some more bad investments.

Did you ever wonder why she fired the house-keeper and maid? Let the gardener go and made do with someone once every couple of weeks? Because she couldn't afford them."

"How did she afford the country club fees, then?" Shelby asked.

"For the last three years Judge Sutherland paid them for her. He died last spring, but there was mention of his gifts in the correspondence Grandmother kept—a favor to an old friend, he termed it."

"Nothing?" Georgia repeated.

"If we can sell the house, we'll be able to pay off the mortgage, with hopefully enough left over for taxes. If we sell the furnishings, that will help pay her last medical bills. Selling her jewelry will get us a bit of cash, but the two necklaces we thought were diamonds are paste—very nice copies, but she apparently sold the originals years ago."

"So that's why she wanted us to marry money," Georgia said slowly.

"No, she always wanted that," Shelby said. "I remember even as a little girl her admonishing me to mind my manners so I could fit in with a certain family."

Margot took a deep breath. "There's more."

Shelby looked at her. "Can't be worse, this has been enough of a shock."

"It doesn't have to do with money. It's about our father."

Georgia and Shelby looked blank.

"Let me guess, he wasn't really married to our mother," Shelby said wryly.

"Actually, he was. Sam Williams."

"Huh?" Georgia asked.

"Didn't you ever wonder why our name was Beaufort, same as Grandmother's?"

"Yes, but I'm with Shelby, though maybe when he cut out Mother found the marriage was bigamous or something and took back her maiden name. Or kept it all along."

"I don't think women did that as much back then. No, I think Grandmother insisted. Just like she did when I left Rand. She very much wanted me to get a divorce, you know. To marry a man fitting the Beaufort name. She was obsessed with the Beaufort name."

"So Sam Williams is dear old daddy," Shelby said scathingly.

"I don't think he left voluntarily," Margot said slowly.

The waitress set their plates on the table, asking if they needed anything else. When she departed, both Georgia and Shelby ignored their meal.

"More," Georgia said.

"I should have told you earlier, but I wanted

to make sure. She rambled in her sleep those last few days before she died. Said all sorts of things. The worst of which was that she had sent Sam packing.''

"Delusional," Georgia said. "I've seen it all the time in the hospital. Doesn't mean anything."

"Maybe not, but added to what else I found, I think it does." Margot related how Harriet had kept Rand and her apart; the letter from Edith she'd found; and repeated as best she could remember her grandmother's exact words.

Stunned, the sisters looked at each other.

"Wow," Shelby said.

"Amen!" said Georgia.

"She was a witch!" Shelby said. "It's unconscionable what she did to you and Rand. I remember how you were hurting when you lost the baby, and how devastated when Rand never called. I'd like to wring her neck!''

Margot nodded. "You can't imagine the rage I felt when I learned. And about our father, too." She looked down at her salad, pushing it around the plate with her fork. "I always thought I'd done something to make him leave."

"That's dumb—and you know it!"

Margot shrugged. "I'm telling you what I thought. I think it made it easier for Harriet to drive a wedge between Rand and me. I guess I sort of expected him to desert me. He just did it earlier than our father.''

''Now what? Is he alive?''

''Who?''

''Our father.''

Margot shrugged. ''I have no idea.''

''I'd like to know. If he is alive, I'd want to ask him why he left,'' Shelby said slowly. ''And why he never came back for us.''

Georgia nodded.

''I think it was something Grandmother did. Once I discover the full story, I guess I'd want to see if we could locate him. Learn what he's been doing all this time. See if he ever missed us,'' Margot said. ''But right now, I'd settle for learning the full story.''

The sisters were silent for a long time. Georgia nibbled a bit of her fish. Shelby drew patterns on the condensation of her glass.

''What next?'' she asked after a long moment.

Margot shook her head. ''I don't know. That's why I wanted to get together. We have to decide how to handle the estate.''

''You wanted to keep the furniture to use in decorating. It would be a great draw,'' Shelby said. ''Selling it immediately won't bring in as much as if you take your time, right?''

''It can't be helped. According to the expenses the lawyer is totaling, the estate owes a lot of money.''

Georgia looked at her shrewdly. ''I bet Rand would help.''

''I'm not asking,'' Margot said firmly.

''Why not?'' Shelby asked. ''He's loaded, if what I hear about him is anything to go by. And I bet he wouldn't mind—especially if you two are getting back together.''

''Oh, right—and have him think that I want to be together for what he can do monetarily?''

''He's not going to think that. The man was crazy about you five years ago, must still be to want you back after all this time. You did leave him, remember,'' Shelby said. ''Ask.''

''No. And I don't need you to tell me what happened five years ago. Do you think I've stopped thinking about it a single day?''

''Just sell the stuff. Get as much as you can for everything and see if it will cover the bills,'' Georgia interjected.

''We could have an estate sale, I suppose,'' Margot said, thinking aloud.

Georgia laughed, the sound infectious. Shelby smiled.

''What?'' Margot asked.

''Won't Grandmother spin in her grave to

know her snooty family was reduced to an estate sale to make ends meet?''

Even Margot smiled.

''That's settled then. I want to hear more about Rand,'' Georgia said.

It was late afternoon by the time Shelby dropped Margot at Rand's condo. She and Georgia had promised to go to Natchez the next weekend to do what they could to hurry the process of closing up Harriet's place. Margot was ready to contact Realtors to list Beaufort Hall, and an auction house to arrange sale of the furnishings. The appraisers were due to finish the next week, so they'd then have an idea of the taxes needed and the total of the bills the attorney was compiling.

On the way back to Rand's place, Margot had Shelby stop at the grocery store. She planned to make Shrimp Creole, one of Rand's favorite meals. Buying all the ingredients, she hesitated buying cooking utensils. Even though he had said he didn't cook much, surely he had the proper implements.

''Are you going to be okay?'' Shelby asked as she pulled into a parking space near Rand's building.

Margot nodded. ''I'm still reeling as I realize the lengths our grandmother went to get her own way. And to keep up appearances. But I'll get through it all. Do you think anyone cared but her?''

''No, not in this day and age. Sell the place, make up with Rand and let's get on with our lives,'' Shelby said.

Rand was not home when Margot let herself in. She experienced a moment of disappointment, but shook it off. He had not known when she was expected back. He'd be along when he finished his meeting.

Busying herself in the kitchen, Margot forgot the cares of the estate and took pleasure in the simple task of cooking. She had loved experimenting with new recipes when they'd been married, relished taking care of her husband. It had been so long, but her contentment increased as the afternoon wore on.

When the Shrimp Creole was simmering, she began to clean up. Rand had plenty of pans and bowls. One she recognized by the chip on the edge. They'd found it at a place near the university on one of their first weekends together. Slowly she dried the bowl, remembering how happy they'd been. Remembering, too, the long, lonely years they'd lived apart. Tears filled her eyes.

She could never get the years back—the time she should have been at Rand's side, helping him, encouraging him and loving him.

A sob escaped. So much time lost. So much love lost.

"Margot?"

Rand turned her around.

She gazed up at him, catching her lower lip between her teeth, blinking the tears from her eyes.

"What is it?" His thumbs brushed her lashes, brushing away the tears. "Did you hurt yourself?"

She shook her head and stepped closer, feeling like she'd come home when his arms drew her into his embrace.

"I missed you," she said, holding on tightly.

"It's only been a few hours," he said, his hands soothing as they rubbed across her back.

She shook her head, leaning into him. "I mean over the last five years. I needed you and turned away. You needed me and I wasn't there." She tried to stem the tears, but they wouldn't stop despite her efforts. "I'd give anything to turn back the clock."

"I know. But it can't be done, Margot. We can only go forward."

She took a deep breath. Decision time.

"Let's go forward—together. I don't think I can bear to be apart another five years," she said, holding him as if she would never let him go.

"That's what we'll do, then," he said.

He kissed her again, and Margot gave back every speck of emotion in her. She wanted to be with him, share his life, learn what was important to him these days, and what he couldn't abide. Wanted to have him to share her days with—and her nights.

She was breathless when he pulled back and gazed into her eyes. Suddenly he smiled, swung her up in his arms and carried her to his bedroom. Setting her on her feet beside the large bed, he looked her frankly in the face.

"No turning back, now, Margot. We go forward right?"

She nodded and reached out to begin to unbutton his shirt, her fingers trembling with the task. She wanted him so much. Loved him so much!

"Together."

It was only as she dished up the Shrimp Creole hours later that Margot realized Rand had not spoken a single word of love. He'd been passionate in bed, driven her to heights never dreamed of. Held her, soothed her, slept with her. But never uttered a single word of love.

To be fair, she'd not said anything, either. But he had to love her, didn't he? He wanted her back, wanted to resume their marriage.

*   *   *

Rand stared out across the river. Night had fallen. In the background he could hear Margot rinsing their dishes. Dinner had been wonderful—one of his favorite meals. When they'd lived together before, she'd made it as a special celebration. Was she celebrating?

He should be. But something nagged him. He'd been concerned when he found her crying this afternoon. The gut-wrenching feeling reminiscent of when she'd cried so much after losing the baby.

But the lovemaking they'd shared in his bed had been stupendous. She'd been open and giving. And the small rituals of domesticity with dinner warmed him. He'd been alone too long. Could they make it last this time?

There was something still not right.

Taking a sip of the cognac in his glass, he realized what it was. Never once had she mentioned the word love.

If she didn't love him, why did she want to resume their marriage?

Had he made a mistake telling her his reason for a divorce? Was she influenced by the thought of the money she'd be entitled to if his company became as large and successful as analysts predicted?

He didn't want to believe that, but it nagged him all the same.

CHAPTER TEN

MARGOT hated to leave New Orleans Sunday night. Rand asked her to stay over, but she had too much to do to let herself be talked into staying.

"The sooner I get things wrapped up in Natchez, the sooner I can move down here," she explained.

"I'll come up on Wednesday and stay the night," he said, kissing her gently.

"I'd like that," she said shyly. Not wanting to cling, almost afraid to let go, she hugged him tightly. "I'll count the minutes until then," she whispered in his ear. She was almost afraid of the newfound happiness. For so long, she'd thought her life would stretch out forever alone and lonely. Now they were being given a second chance. It was almost too wonderful to trust.

"Drive carefully," he said gruffly, kissing her long and hard.

Monday Margot contacted an estate auction

sales office and a Realtor and made arrangements with both.

Tuesday she discussed her plans with her small staff, and spoke with her assistant in private to see if the woman wanted to go into partnership. When Jessie excitedly agreed, Margot knew at least one phase of her relocation would go smoothly. She hated not being able to wind up Harriet's estate while she stayed in Natchez, but couldn't wait to move back with Rand.

Tuesday she also returned to Beaufort Hall. She'd read all the correspondence and found nothing further relating to her father. Proof apparently wasn't going to be found in Harriet's papers. But Margot knew in her heart. To see the truth in black and white would have been nice, but after what Harriet had done between her and Rand, she knew her grandmother had been instrumental in driving away her father. She didn't know how, or why, but she no longer needed the proof she had once so longed for.

"More mail came since you were here last," Caroline said when Margot sat down for dinner. The older woman plopped a stack of envelopes, flyers and catalogs down beside Margot's place. "Eat first before reading."

Margot nodded and waited until Caroline had returned to the kitchen. Slowly, while eating, she sifted through the mail. Not much worth even looking at. She received some of the same catalogs at her place.

There was a letter with shaky writing addressed to Harriet Beaufort's Granddaughters.

Intrigued, Margot opened it. A sympathy card. From Edith Strong!

She stared at it, a strange premonition taking hold. Was this the same Edith of the letter from so long ago?

Looking at the return address, Margot noted it was a retirement home not too far from Natchez.

Not waiting to finish her meal, she dashed to the phone.

"Marstall," Rand's deep voice immediately filled her with delight.

Feeling almost giddy, she smiled. "Hi, it's Margot. Guess what I just got?"

"A winning lottery ticket worth ten million dollars if the excitement in your voice is to be believed," he said.

"Better than that! Remember the letter from Edith—the one that made mention of Harriet's interfering?"

"Yes."

"I think I have a card from that same Edith— a sympathy card on the loss of our grandmother. Rand—she's living in a retirement home not too far from Natchez."

"And you want to go see her," he guessed.

She laughed, giddy with excitement. "Yes! Maybe she can tell me what I need to know."

"Tomorrow, we'll go tomorrow when I get there. Wait for me. I'll arrive around one, all right?"

Margot didn't want to wait another minute, but she knew a few more hours wouldn't matter—not after all this time. And she'd like to have Rand with her.

"Okay, I'll wait. Pick me up at the shop. And don't be late."

"I won't. I want to see you," he said in a low tone.

Margot felt her bones melt. She leaned against the wall and closed her eyes against the longing that filled her. "I want to see you, too. Yesterday and today seemed endless!"

"Tomorrow, then."

"Keep safe." She hung up the phone. He'd be with her tomorrow! She wished he would stay until she could move to New Orleans, but knew that was wishful thinking on a grand scale. She would be content with whatever time they could snatch together before her move. After all, it was so much more than she'd had over the last few years!

Edith was almost forgotten as Margot anticipated Rand's arrival. She'd missed him. More these last couple of days than in the last five years, she believed. The weekend had proved to her that they belonged together. And she was willing to take him on whatever terms he dictated. If he didn't love her anymore, it was her own fault. She loved him enough for both of them.

And talking on the phone wasn't enough. She wanted him with her, wanted to be with him!

Grateful the baby issue had been shelved, she wouldn't bring it up. They could be happy the two of them, without a baby. It wasn't the life they'd originally planned so long ago, but it would work. She'd do her damnedest to make it work.

Wednesday, Margot rose, excitement and a hint of trepidation churning in her stomach. The thought of coffee almost made her sick. She needed something to soothe her overwrought nerves, not exacerbate them. Rand would be in Natchez soon, only a few more hours! Eating dry toast and some tea, she hurried impatiently through breakfast and left for the office.

She took the sympathy card and envelope with her to work. Each time a client walked in she looked up, hoping Rand might arrive early.

When Jessie suggested she grab a quick bite, Margot shook her head. She didn't feel a bit like eating. Her stomach still churned with excitement, with anticipation. Maybe she'd find out the truth today about her father and what her grandmother had done.

And if not, she wasn't going to worry about it any longer. Rand was more important. She wanted to concentrate her attention on him!

Rand didn't arrive until after one. He breezed into the shop and seemed to fill it.

Margot grabbed her purse and almost ran the short distance to greet him.

"Hi," she said breathlessly.

"Hi yourself," He leaned over to kiss her, noting the excitement in her eyes. For him? Or for her quest? Maybe today she'd find out the truth about what Harriet had done. He hoped knowing would bring her the resolution she sought.

"Hmm," she said, giving in to the kiss. "I've missed you. It was awful to be apart, but the getting back together isn't bad," she murmured.

His arms tightened around her. He liked the way she thought.

"Let's go find your grandmother's friend." The sooner the task was completed, the sooner he could have her alone.

"And hope she remembers," Margot said, waving a farewell to her assistant.

The drive to the retirement home was short. Before long they parked adjacent to the beautiful grounds of Sunny Acres. Walking up the wide sidewalk, Margot felt almost sick. She swallowed hard, hoping she could find the end to the puzzle here. If not, would she give up her quest? Was being back with Rand enough? Her mother and father would never have that opportunity. She did, and still couldn't believe her good fortune.

They were shown in to a bright parlor and in only a few minutes a lady arrived pushed in a wheelchair.

"Edith Strong?" Margot asked, standing and crossing to the elderly woman, offering her hand.

"Yes. I don't get visitors very often. Who are you?" She looked older than Harriet had, her hair entirely white, wispy and thin. Her eyes peered up at Margot through thick glasses.

"I'm Margot Beaufort—Harriet Beaufort's granddaughter. One of them. I received your card yesterday."

Edith shook her head and motioned for Margot to sit on the nearby chair. "I thought for sure I'd go before Harriet. Fell and broke my hip four years ago. Won't ever walk again, you know. Most old folks like me don't get up and about after something like that. But

Harriet—she had so daggum much determination that I thought she'd outlive us all." She shook her head again.

"You and she were friends," Margot said, sitting on the edge of the chair. Impatiently she wanted to find out everything. But kept her voice calm. Rand leaned against the wall a few steps away, quietly watching. She flicked him a glance and then looked back at Edith.

"We were good friends for a long time." Her expression became pensive. "Weathered a lot of ups and downs, I can tell you."

"Was one of the downs when she drove my father away?" Margot asked gently.

Edith looked at her sharply. "Know about that, do you?"

Margot nodded. "Not the details, though. Could you fill those in?"

Edith gazed off into the distance for a long time, then sighed softly and began to speak. "I told her at the time she was a fool to do it. It isn't right that a person play God that away. And once her Amanda died, I think she regretted what she'd done. Amanda would be alive today, I believe, if Harriet hadn't interfered. But her pride was something awful, and her determination to get what she wanted. Only time I've seen her shaken and furious was when Amanda came home after marrying Sam Williams."

"My parents were married a number of years. How could Harriet have driven my father away?" Margot asked.

"Amanda married him in New Orleans. He was an oil wildcatter—worked the rigs in the gulf. They had you almost before Harriet knew they'd been married. I suspected Amanda wasn't chancing anything going wrong. She didn't want to do anything but be married to Sam. He was a fine figure of a man—tall, broad shouldered. Dark hair." She glanced at Margot, "You've the look of him, a bit. And he sure adored you. Many's the time I was at Harriet's when your father tossed you up in the air, laughing with you, claiming you were his sunshine."

Margot swallowed hard. *Her father had loved her!* He hadn't wanted to leave.

"What happened?"

"Tom Prescott's what happened," Edith snapped.

"Who is Tom Prescott?" Margot recognized the name—the Prescotts were an old Mississippi family—with a fortune from cotton and rice.

"He was a young man who became smitten with your mother. And he came from the background Harriet wanted for Amanda—old family, old money. Not some jumped up, no-account wildcatter.'' Edith peered at Margot.

"Harriet did all she could to throw Tom and Amanda together—to no avail, Amanda had eyes only for her Sam. So Harriet trumped up charges against your father for the murder of an old man in Natchez County. Got old Judge Sutherland to help her. He'd wanted to marry your grandmother for years. She didn't want to give up the Beaufort name, but wasn't above using his devotion when it suited her.''

"They accused my father of *murder*?''

"She met with Sam privately—swore she had proof that would convict him, and that she'd use it if he didn't leave. Had the judge issue a warrant and everything. Quiet like, though. Didn't want her name dragged in the mud. I don't know what that proof was, but it must have been pretty strong. Sam left to protect his family and Amanda soon died of a broken heart. She was pregnant with that third girl, what's her name?''

"Georgia.''

"Georgia. That's right. Don't think Sam even knew there was another one on the way. He lit out and we never heard from him again. Of course your mother died soon after that third girl was born. Don't know if he heard about it or not, but if he did, maybe he felt there was no reason to return.''

Her eyes shifted as if she gazed into the distant past. ''They were a fine young couple, so in love, so happy. Harriet couldn't stand that, you know. She wanted her Amanda allied with the Prescotts. Instead the girl died young. Harriet never said another word about Sam. But I sure have wondered over the years how much she must have regretted what she'd done.''

''There were reasons to return, his daughters!'' Margot said.

''Honey, he knew that harridan of a grandmother of yours would slap him in jail so fast it'd make your head spin. He didn't have the money or resources to fight a Beaufort.

''I told her she'd done a terrible thing. But she wanted that Tom Prescott for Amanda and wouldn't be stopped.''

''Instead Mama died,'' Margot said softly.

''She sure did. That was a sad day. And it knocked Harriet for a loop. But she rallied and said she'd have three chances now to do the Beauforts proud. She had three granddaughters.''

''None of us married to suit her, either.'' She glanced at Rand. ''But not for lack of trying on her part. Wouldn't you have thought she'd learn from what happened with her daughter?''

"No, child. I surely wouldn't. She was one determined woman. I wrote her once about it...she was never the same friend afterward. I moved to Santee a few years after. Our friendship dwindled. But I was truly sorry when I heard of her death a few days ago. We were girls together, you know. Don't have many friends left who remember when we were girls," Edith said.

Rand didn't say anything as he walked beside Margot to the car. He tried to imagine how she felt. He was furious with Harriet, not only for the separation she fostered between him and Margot, but for the three little girls who had been denied a father's love and support during their growing years. All for her own idea of what her daughter's life should be.

"Are you all right?" he asked as she stopped by the car door.

She nodded and looked up at him.

"I'm sad for my parents. They got a raw deal from Harriet. But, Rand, my father didn't desert us! He was driven away. A murder charge would be enough to drive anyone away and keep him away. I wonder what happened to the warrant? Is there still one out for my father?"

"We can check in with the local police and find out." He lightly touched her shoulder. "I'm glad you let me come with you."

She nodded. "I almost didn't, I was so impatient this morning, but figured I might need the moral support."

"And I can give you that?"

"That and a lot more," she said, reaching up to brush her lips across his cheek. "I can't wait to call Georgia and Shelby and let them know."

"What next?"

"Home, I guess. Unless you want to stop at the police station first?"

"Might as well get it all cleared up this afternoon. Are you going to pursue this?"

"Pursue what?" she asked.

"Finding your father."

"I hadn't thought that far ahead. Actually just finding out the truth is enough for now. Though I guess it would be interesting to find him. To learn what he's done over the years. And let him know his daughters are doing all right."

The stop at the police station turned up no warrants for Sam Williams. They could discover no sign that one had ever been issued, so there was no way to tell if Harriet's threat had been empty, or if Judge Sutherland had rescinded it long ago.

On a hunch, Rand drove to the library. Looking through back issues of the *Natchez*

Record, they found an article concerning a death of an old itinerant laborer. And another one several months later announced that the killer had been apprehended. The date of that paper was shortly after Amanda's death. If nothing else, the warrant would have had to be rescinded then.

Margot flipped off the microfilm reader after rewinding the film.

"It's so sad," she said softly, looking at Rand. She reached out and touched him lightly. "And history almost repeated itself with us, didn't it?"

He reached for her hand, bringing it to his lips and kissing her palm. "Almost. Harriet was a dangerous woman!

"Your apartment or the Hall?" he asked as they left the library.

"The Hall. Caroline knew you were coming and is preparing another elaborate dinner for us."

"Sounds good."

"Just don't get used to such fancy meals. I won't have as much time to spend on cooking while I'm starting my new branch in New Orleans."

"Eating comes a mighty long way down the list," he said, reaching over to take her hand, lacing his fingers with hers.

Rand's cell phone rang just as they arrived at Beaufort Hall. He spoke into it as Margot indicated she'd go on inside. Hurrying up the stairs, she wanted to change into something more comfortable than her suit. She wouldn't mind taking a brief nap, she felt tired and drained. Learning the history of her parents' brief marriage and ending had been almost more than she could stand. She had to call her sisters, but would do so later. Lying down, she closed her eyes. She'd rest just for a moment and then call Shelby and Georgia.

"Miss Margot, dinner is ready," Caroline said, leaning over her and shaking her shoulder gently.

Margot opened her eyes. Instead of resting, she'd fallen sound asleep!

"And you best look to finding Mr. Rand. He was wandering around the downstairs rooms for a while. I saw him in the study. But now I don't know where he is. I don't want dinner to get cold!"

Margot quickly brushed her hair and donned a light sundress, then ran lightly down the steps. She peeked into every room on the ground floor, but didn't find Rand.

Going out on the veranda, she looked around

the yard. There—in the distance on the levee he walked with his hands in his pocket.

She called to Caroline that she'd be right back and started off to intercept him.

Smiling happily, she didn't realize at first he didn't reciprocate.

"Hi," she said as she drew close. Her eyes searched his face. He looked tired. An early night for them would set things to right.

Rand said nothing, just looked at her, his face impassive.

Oh-oh, Margot thought, now what? Her heart began to beat heavily. Had he received bad news? Had another tanker run aground?

"Caroline has dinner ready," she said brightly.

"I won't be staying for dinner."

"What's wrong?" The smile faded. His gaze was hard, direct.

"You tell me, Margot." He stepped closer and gripped her arms. "When did you plan to tell me about your grandmother's debts?"

Margot stared at him, slowly licking her dry lips. Her heart raced. Heat washed through her. "I don't know that I ever was," she said slowly. "It doesn't concern you, just my sisters and me."

"Didn't you think I would find it interesting that you decided to resume this marriage just when I'm poised to make a huge profit by taking the company the next step and at a time when your own personal fortune has vanished?"

"You think I wanted to come back because of money?" she asked, hurt he'd ever suspect her of such a thing. Yet hadn't she withheld the information for that very fear?

"You're good with that disingenuous display of amazement."

His words hurt. But Margot drew on her resources. "The only amazement is that I even considered resuming a marriage with you! Not only are you a workaholic caring more for business than your family, you're paranoid to boot."

"When did you find out?" he asked sharply.

She hesitated, then raised her chin. "Two weeks ago. Harriet's attorney called me in. That's the reason I had to meet with my sisters when I was in New Orleans. It impacts them. And me. But not you." She broke his hold and stepped back. "How did you find out?"

"Your attorney called this afternoon. When you didn't respond to Caroline's call, I took it."

"You should have taken a message."

"The timing of this reconciliation seems mighty convenient to me, don't you think? I foolishly try to establish a base of honesty by telling you about the company's expansion plans. You still hold me off, but once you learn of your grandmother's lack of money, suddenly you want to move back. Suddenly it's a good idea to resume our marriage.''

Margot felt sick. He interpreted everything wrong. Her grandmother's estate, or lack of one, had nothing to do with her wanting to start over with Rand. Hadn't he felt any of the attraction she felt? She loved him, hadn't he felt even a glimmer of that?

No, he had never said a word about love or caring.

''If that's what you believe,'' she said tightly, ''please leave.''

''Can you offer another scenario? Want to explain the timing if nothing else?''

She tightened her lips and shook her head. The last thing she would do is argue. The hurt pierced as sharp as last time. She'd thought they'd been given a second chance. Now she knew she'd been fooling herself. There were no second chances.

For once her grandmother had been correct. She should have divorced the man many years ago and gotten on with her life.

''I don't have to justify my actions to you. If you can't take my word that money has nothing to do with us, then I think we are better off apart.''

Sweep me into your arms, tell me you love me, that money doesn't matter at all!

But Rand made no move to touch her. Without another word, he walked away.

Margot went to bed without eating that night, lay awake staring at the darkness for hours. Her nap had robbed her of the fatigue she needed to sleep. And Rand's parting words echoed over and over in her mind, keeping her restless and awake. How could he have thought that about her? How could he think she only wanted his money?

The next day Margot collected all the papers she needed from Harriet's desk. She walked through the house one last time and marked the items for each of her sisters and herself.

She gave Caroline instructions on keeping the house dusted and aired out each day until the estate sale, then left. She had no intention of returning until the day of the sale. And maybe not even then, if one of her sisters could do it.

Refusing to think about Rand, she swung by the office. But her lack of sleep was catching up with her, as was her refusal to eat. She felt queasy and tired, disheartened. She made an excuse to Jessie and left for home. She'd have to go through with the partnership; she couldn't disappoint her assistant. But there would be no new branch in New Orleans.

Saturday Margot slept in late. Feeling refreshed when she woke, she called Shelby and told her not to come. She also told her about meeting with Edith and asked her to call Georgia.

"Things okay, Margot?" Shelby asked.

"Sure, what's not to be okay?" Margot tried flippantly. But she must not have been successful.

"I don't know, but you sound upset."

"Wouldn't you be to find out our father was driven away by the machinations of a manipulative old woman? And Edith thought our mother died of a broken heart!"

"It was the flu," Shelby said. "Grandmother told us that often enough."

"But if a person has no will to live, they give in to illnesses that would not ordinarily affect them."

"Now you sound like Georgia."

"You don't have to be a nurse to know that."

"So what's next?"

"The estate sale will be within the month. I marked the furniture we each wanted. The appraisers are finished. The tax bill will be forthcoming soon, I'm sure. I think I have a full recount of the medical—''

''Margot, what's with you and Rand? Will you be there to handle all that, or be living here by then?''

Margot pressed against the pain in her heart. Swallowing, she desperately tried for control. She would not let that man get to her a second time. Taking a shaky breath, she tried to keep her voice even.

''Rand and I are not resuming our marriage after all.''

Quickly getting off the phone, Margot was surprised at how much the statement hurt. Better get used to it, girl, she admonished herself. She'd done it once before, she could do it again.

Monday she received a letter from Rand's attorneys, and the divorce papers.

Tearing them up, she placed them in an envelope and mailed them back. Angry at the callous way he proceeded, she fumed all afternoon.

She ought to teach him a lesson. She was not the money grasper he thought, but maybe she should give him a taste of that. Maybe she should show the man she wasn't easily pushed aside.

Tuesday afternoon Rand called at the shop.

Jessie answered and when she told Margot who was calling, she refused the call.

Margot had been upset when he'd accused her of wanting him solely for his money. Now she was downright angry.

A registered letter arrived on Thursday—another letter from Rand's attorneys and a new set of divorce papers. Instead of tearing these up, she read them. Furious anew, Margot began to make plans.

Friday, she made two appointments. By that afternoon her head was reeling. She had had enough. Tomorrow morning, early, she was heading for New Orleans to see Rand. To finalize things once and for all.

Margot parked across the street from Rand's building, considering it a good omen. At the lobby door, she started to ring the downstairs bell. Then hesitated. Rummaging in her purse, she found the key he'd given her. Opening the heavy glass door, she sailed up to his apartment without a qualm. The next few minutes would determine her life once and for all. Odd, she felt calm and controlled. She should be ranting and raving and scared to death. Maybe that would all come later.

But for now, she wasn't some young twenty-year-old anymore. Her grandmother was no longer in the picture. For better or worse, she was on her own now. But it could be some of Harriet's determination had shown up in her oldest granddaughter.

She opened his apartment and slipped inside, listening. The aroma of fresh coffee filled the air. She heard the rustle of a newspaper from the kitchen. He was probably eating breakfast. She glanced at her watch—at 9:34 in the morning? He should have been at work hours ago, never mind that it was Saturday. She'd planned to stop here first and then check at his office.

Slowly she walked to the kitchen door and stopped, the sight of him unexpectedly surprising her. He looked tired—lines bracketed his mouth that hadn't been there a few days ago. He hadn't shaved yet. The sweats he wore were baggy and old. The man was worth a ton of money and still wore old baggy sweats from five years ago?

Though she didn't move or make a sound, he looked up suddenly, froze. Slowly he lowered the paper.

Boldly Margot raised her chin and crossed the room. "I have two things to say to you. Depending on how you react, we will end this foolishness one way or the other."

"What foolishness?"

Even his voice had a disturbing effect on her

nerves. Her knees felt wobbly, but she would not sit down. Standing gave her the power position.

Opening her purse, she drew out the divorce papers—and the additional sheet her attorney had prepared.

"I will tell you this only once. You can accept it or not. If not, then I will sign the papers you so kindly sent—with this one additional one that says you relinquish everything that is mine. I want nothing from you, Rand, and I expect you to sign this sheet relinquishing anything of mine of which I now possess."

His eyes narrowed as he studied her. "Go on."

She took a deep breath—now or never!

"I love you," she said baldly. "I realize that I haven't told you that in five years. I don't know how you feel, but I wanted you to know that I love you. I have from almost the first day we met. I probably will until the day I die. I agreed to resume our marriage for the sole reason that I love you. I wanted to be with you. We were young when tragedy hit, and we didn't know how to cope. I've learned coping techniques over the years but that changed nothing. I still feel as strongly about you as ever. I never got a divorce, never dated other men, never wanted anyone but you in all my life."

"And our baby."

She nodded. "That goes without saying." She took a deep breath. "Whether you believe me or not is up to you. But it was never about money. Not for me."

Slowly he rose, took a step that placed him right in front of her.

The back of his fingers brushed against her cheek, the hard glint in his eye belying the gentleness of his touch. "And if I say I don't believe you?"

CHAPTER ELEVEN

"THEN I'll sign the papers here and now, as long as you agree to the additional term that my attorney prepared," she said evenly.

Rand tried to ignore the surge of feelings that filled him with her declaration of love. He'd never loved anyone as intensely, as completely as he had Margot Beaufort. He'd been so long without her, he actually thought he could live the rest of his life and never see her again. These last few days had proved him wrong. He'd missed her with a longing that scared him. She was right: they'd been young when they'd first married, and he'd been bent on proving to himself and to the world he could succeed. But at what cost? He didn't want to be alone; he wanted Margot in his life.

Did she really love him? Looking into her eyes convinced him—if he had ever truly doubted it.

Despite the interference of her grandmother, despite the years apart, despite the misunderstanding and evidence to the contrary, he believed her.

Slowly he cupped her face. ''I love you, Margot.''

She released her breath in a whoosh and clung to his wrists.

''Oh, God! I was bluffing,'' she confessed. ''I don't think I could have walked away no matter what you said.''

''Good bluff.'' He lowered his head and kissed her, drawing her tightly into his arms where she belonged. The feel of her body set his afire. Her scent sparked memories and desire. Her warmth lit a conflagration, and the way she returned his kiss told him he had found true love. They'd sort the rest out later. For now he just wanted to hold her, love her.

A long time later Rand lifted his head, taking in her flushed cheeks, the stars that seemed to shine in her eyes, the damp, slightly swollen lips that had so passionately returned his kisses.

''You said you had two things to say. Before we move into another area of the apartment, what's the second?''

Swallowing hard, she tilted her head, as if trying to judge his reaction.

''It can't be bad,'' he offered. ''Haven't we got the worst behind us yet?''

She shook her head. "I was afraid to come here today, but I was so angry with you, it gave me false courage." She hesitated. "But I'm even more afraid about being pregnant," she said in a rush.

The familiar pain struck. He wanted kids. He wanted to give them the love his parents had given him, but provide more for them than he'd had as a child. He wanted to spend lazy vacations at the beach, or the mountains. Teach them to play ball, and to enjoy fine music. But if it wasn't to be, he could live with that. He knew Margot had suffered terribly with the miscarriage—only now was he coming to understand the full extent. Taking a deep breath, he rested his forehead against hers.

"Then we won't get pregnant," he said slowly, relinquishing a dream. He wanted Margot, on whatever terms she stated.

"Oh, Rand!" She laughed up at him even as tears welled in her eyes. "That's so sweet, but a little late. I *am* pregnant."

"What?" Shock coursed through him.

She nodded, the tears brimming over. "I had it confirmed yesterday—it must have been that very first time." She blushed slightly. "I think we must have forgotten to take precautions. But I'm still scared to death. My doctor said it should be all right, but what if it isn't? I don't think I could bear it.''

"You're pregnant?"

She nodded, smiling despite the tears, which he tried to brush away. Astonishment gave way to incredulity, then a deep abiding happiness. It was as if they were starting over, past and present merging to forge the strong future they once hoped to have.

"I'll see nothing happens to you this time, Margot. I promise!"

"Knowing I have your love will be enough. We'll make it this time." She reached up and kissed him.

"What?" He was more attuned to her than he thought. He could tell she had more to say. For a moment fear clutched him. Was there something she hadn't told him? Something serious, about her own health, or the pregnancy?

"Is there something wrong? Something I need to know?"

She shook her head, her smile wobbly.

"There is something, tell me."

"Would you think me really silly to want to get married again? I mean, I know we've been married all along, but somehow, this feels like starting over. Like it's all new. I don't know, I just thought driving down that if we started

over, we could do it with a proper wedding and
a renewal of our vows.''

''So you could wear a white dress and veil?''
He smiled, imagining her walking down the
church aisle toward him.

''Hardly white, and it doesn't need to be
elaborate. But maybe a nice dress and hat?''

''I'd love to see you walk down the aisle to
me! I would love to renew our vows—in front
of God and all our friends this time. We'll do
it up right. No courthouse this time, but your
church. With your sisters there, and all our
friends. My mom will love the idea. I don't
think you're being silly, sweetheart. I think it's
a great plan. And it would make it twice as hard
to ever separate again.''

Three months later.

''You look beautiful,'' Shelby said, fussing
with the roses in Margot's hair.

''Well I feel like a blimp,'' Margot com-
plained, turning sideways to the mirror. The soft
swell of her belly hardly extended enough to
disrupt the flow of the lovely lace and satin pale
blue-colored dress. The inverted pleat on the
short skirt gave way enough to let the whole
world know she was pregnant. She smiled despite her complaint.

"A bride isn't supposed to be four months' pregnant."

"No, but a wife can be." Impulsively Shelby hugged her sister. "I'm so happy for you. And look on the bright side. This time you get to be a June bride."

Margot returned the hug, smiling broadly. "We barely made it into June. We were lucky the church was available this first weekend. I'm more thankful the morning sickness is behind me."

"It sure would look silly to have the bride interrupt the ceremony while she took a mad dash to the bathroom," Georgia agreed, handing Margot the lovely bouquet of pale pink roses Rand had sent. Matching corsages were already pinned to her shoulder and Shelby's.

"Half of Natchez is out there, I swear," Shelby said a minute later peeking out to the church. It was the same one she and her sisters had attended all their lives. The one Harriet had planned to have each granddaughter marry in. At least that part of the old woman's schemes was coming true. Only she would have thought the man wrong. But Margot knew Harriet was the one who would have been wrong. Rand was perfect. Anyone who saw them together knew that.

"It was nice of you to send a car for Edith

Strong,'' Georgia said, fussing with her own hair, giving up with a sigh.

"She's a nice woman, and I'm grateful for her telling me the truth about what happened with our father.''

"You never carried it any further. Want to?'' Shelby asked casually.

"What do you mean?

"I mean knowing he didn't leave us of his own volition, is that enough?''

Margot nodded. "For now at least. He didn't abandon us, he was driven away. Nothing can change that, you know. We grew up without a father, without a mother. I would change things if I could, but I can't, so I'm making sure this next generation has both parents,'' she said firmly, placing her hand protectively over the mound of her stomach.

"Besides, what do you suggest I do? The man's been gone for twenty-three years, has probably built himself a new life—and who could blame him? But he could be anywhere in the world, and I have a branch office to open, a new house to decorate and a husband who is proving to be very demanding.''

She smiled, not that she would have it any other way. Rand had taken to bringing work home, and then abandoning it to spend the time with her. His workaholic ways had changed drastically. And she knew she could count on him to be with her whenever she needed him in the future. That had been another promise.

"They're starting the wedding march," Georgia said. She hugged her older sister. "Be happy!"

"How can I help it with Rand?"

Her sisters flanking her, Margot started down the aisle to the man whom she would always love.

Arriving at his side, she reached for his hand, just as she felt a flutter of life deep inside. They'd come full circle. But they were stronger now, and could manage whatever life threw their way—together. Today would seal that promise!

"I love you," she whispered as the pastor took his place before them.

"I love you, too, Margot, and always will," Rand replied, leaning over to kiss her before the ceremony began.

HARLEQUIN PRESENTS®

The world's bestselling romance series...
The series that brings you your favorite authors,
month after month:

Helen Bianchin...Emma Darcy
Lynne Graham...Penny Jordan
Miranda Lee...Sandra Morton
Anne Mather...Carole Mortimer
Susan Napier...Michelle Reid

and many more uniquely talented authors!

Wealthy, powerful, gorgeous men...
Women who have feelings just like your own...
The stories you love, set in exotic, glamorous locations...

HARLEQUIN PRESENTS,
Seduction and passion guaranteed!

Visit us at www.romance.net

HPGEN99

Harlequin® Historical

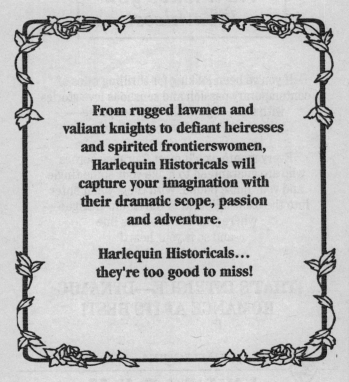

From rugged lawmen and
valiant knights to defiant heiresses
and spirited frontierswomen,
Harlequin Historicals will
capture your imagination with
their dramatic scope, passion
and adventure.

Harlequin Historicals...
they're too good to miss!

HHGENR

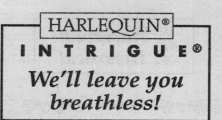

Romance is just one click away!

online book serials

> ➤ *Exclusive* to our web site, get caught up in both the daily and weekly online installments of new romance stories.

> ➤ Try the Writing Round Robin. Contribute a chapter to a story created by our members. Plus, winners will get prizes.

romantic travel

> ➤ Want to know where the best place to kiss in New York City is, or which restaurant in Los Angeles is the most romantic? Check out our Romantic Hot Spots for the scoop.

> ➤ Share your travel tips and stories with us on the romantic travel message boards.

romantic reading library

> ➤ Relax as you read our collection of Romantic Poetry.

> ➤ Take a peek at the Top 10 Most Romantic Lines!

Visit us online at

www.eHarlequin.com
on Women.com Networks